THE WILD BOAR

THE WILD BOAR

FELIX METTLER

Translated from the German by
EDNA McCOWN

Fromm International Publishing Corporation
NEW YORK

Grateful acknowledgment is made to Pro Helvetia,
the Swiss Council for the Arts,
for its support of this work.
Translation copyright © 1992
Fromm International Publishing Corporation, New York

Originally published in 1990 as *Der Keiler*
Copyright © 1990, Ammann Verlag AG, Zürich,
Switzerland

Printed in the United States of America

First U.S. Edition

Library of Congress Cataloging-in-Publication Data

Mettler, Felix, 1945-
[Keiler. English]
The wild boar / Felix Mettler ; translated from the
German by Edna McCown.—1st U.S. ed.
p.   cm.
Translation of: Der Keiler.
ISBN 0-88064-134-7 (hardback : acid-free paper) : $18.95
I. Title.
PT2673.E853K413   1992
833'.914—dc20   91-38835 CIP

ISBN 0-88064-134-7

For Simone

1

Gottfried Sonder climbed the narrow steps that connected the bus stop with St. Stephan's Clinic. They led through an ancient stand of dark firs, the trunks covered with black-green moss—thin-needled tamaracks, birches, beech trees, and elms—relics of a once-splendid park. Long, leafy branches partially shaded the steps and the morning sun slanted through the thick foliage, forming a pattern of dancing points of light on the ground. The trees muffled the noise of the city and reminded Sonder of a quiet forest; the shadows were refreshingly cool, he thought he could smell mossy forest earth. This would have evoked a longing in him once. Even a few months ago.

Sonder took each step slowly, deliberately, almost as if his feet were fighting the stairs. But had he been asked, he would have been incapable of saying why, or what he felt. He might have said he didn't want to run short of breath or his scar would start hurting again, or that he didn't want to break out in a sweat. It was already warm, unseasonably warm for a spring morning in Zurich. But probably he would have replied that he was tired, simply tired. One would have believed whatever he said.

At the top of the steps a massive fir—it was a

Wellington—rose high up into the cloudless sky. Sonder stopped beside the tree, as he always did when he had not been to work for a few days, and gazed over the city and the lake, shining silver, behind which the Alps could be seen, still covered in snow.

He noticed the numerous brightly colored cranes that stood among the buildings, towering over them like huge wading birds, singly or in groups. Weren't they proof that everything could be replaced? Or almost everything. The steeples and domes, he told himself, were the same as in old pictures of the city. Even the churches and government buildings, the guildhalls and the university remained the same as before, forever unchanged, and not only from a distance.

There were hardly any construction sites in Venice, it occurred to him; all the buildings were falling apart at the same pace, the churches and palaces as well, plaster crumbled everywhere, water was washing everything away. The shiny black gondolas with their metal fittings and plastic flowers had reminded him of coffins. But he had found Venice fascinating despite this, or because of it. He had visited the city for a few days after the date for his operation had been scheduled. Venice without all of that, without the omnipresent decay, the musty smell, the threat of sinking, would be unimaginable, he thought, probably insufferable. The coffin-shaped gondolas were part of it as well; they belonged to the city, a city obviously dedicated to total ruin. Unlike Zurich, for the most part, the cranes were a testimony to that.

The sun was already quite strong, unusually bright for this time of day; there was something ominous about it that made Sonder think of Africa. The meteorological institute for weeks had been reporting a stable high-pressure area over Central Europe. It was going to be as hot as a summer day. There was a forest-fire warning for the northern Alps.

Sonder took a few steps toward the huge trunk of the tree and ran his splayed fingers over the rugged bark. He admired the giant, standing as if it had always stood there and would stand there forever. A sanctuary, like the churches and the guildhalls. His sanctuary. The fact that the tree was rotten from within and could fall at the first autumn storm was something Sonder had never considered before.

A bit farther up the three white, almost cubical buildings of St. Stephan's Clinic came into view. They were staggered along the edge of the woods, connected by glass passageways. Gardeners were dragging hoses across the landscaped meadow in front of the buildings, crisscrossed by a number of paths—all wheelchair accessible, of course. The earth was so dry it was cracked, and the flowers were threatening to wilt prematurely.

The Department of Pathology was located in the last of the three buildings. Sonder had worked there performing autopsies since the clinic had opened in the late fifties. Today, without thinking, he took a path he seldom followed, a roundabout way to his workplace. Sonder barely noticed his surroundings, neither the ornamental shrubbery along the paths nor the laurel-wreathed busts of various physicians. He saw only the gravel of the path, disappearing under his faltering steps.

Actually, Gottfried Sonder seemed quite healthy; his face and his strong hands were tanned by the sun. Only those who knew him well noticed the changes in him, his strange posture. And it had become more obvious that he dragged his right leg, the result of an old encounter with a wild boar. The doctor in Davos, where he had spent four weeks in a sanatorium, was of the opinion

3

that he had recovered well, and had noted in his report that his incision had healed without complications and that his lungs were functioning normally again. But what does that really mean? Sonder thought. He felt empty, hollowed out, as if they had cut away more than just a piece of his lung. But he couldn't say that to a doctor; it was his problem and he would have to deal with it himself.

He had one more month of work, then he would retire. Only one month more, and he would be free, absolutely free. His pension and his meager savings would have been enough to enable him to carry out his plans, would have allowed him to do what he had dreamed of for such a long time. And now this. True, they said he was healthy, but he could guess what was to come. At least he believed he could. There were statistics on the various kinds of cancer, percentages on survival rates—for one year, for three years, or five. He knew them, had become familiar with them over the years. He knew only too well what a recurrence or a metastasis could mean. A little cough could be proof enough of how far along it was, or a slight pain, or shortness of breath. At any time.

Passing through the entrance gate, Sonder nodded to Frau Moosbacher, a plump, red-faced woman who was sitting as usual behind the pane of glass. And he was surprised that she smiled and nodded to him as always, as if nothing had changed, as if he were the same man who had appeared for work here for years. She must know what had happened to him, he thought, must know very well. A thing like that gets around.

Sonder hastened his step when he saw the empty corridor before him, and reached the changing room without encountering anyone. He hoped that his work clothes would make him feel more assured. But someone else's things were hanging in his locker. The label on the door said O. Zimmerli. Sonder immediately closed the locker and stood for a while before it, holding on to it with outstretched arms. Of course. He should have known. After all, they needed someone to take over his job in a month. Nevertheless! He was here, ready to work, and no one expected him. Why not? What was it the doctors knew? What were they keeping from him?

Sonder defiantly slammed the flat of his hand against the locker door and sank down onto the bench as the ringing sound of metal faded in the room. He stared at the floor, thinking of nothing, incapable of forming one concrete thought. And suddenly faces leaped at him from the leaden, bluish-gray flagstones and grimaced at him, faces with bulbous noses, with one eye, all grinning at him spitefully. Shapes appeared, hunchbacked, club-footed gnomes that slowly began to move. And when Sonder closed his eyes to banish the sinister images, the shapes turned into people, flesh-and-blood people who danced around, mocking him.

Fifteen minutes, a half hour must have passed before a stranger approached Sonder, an almost delicate-looking man with pomaded black hair and a thin little moustache. He could have been Italian. Or Spanish perhaps.

"Herr Sonder, isn't it?" The man spoke Swiss German without an accent.

Sonder nodded.

"Zimmerli, Oskar Zimmerli."

"Pleased to meet you," Sonder said mechanically. He had pictured his successor differently, certainly sturdier.

"They gave me your locker," Zimmerli said. "I'm sorry. Doctor Götze said you weren't coming back to work."

5

"He did, did he?"

"I don't know where your lab coat is. I'm sorry."

"It's all right," Sonder countered. Why should Zimmerli apologize? It wasn't his fault.

"Should I inform Professor Bäni that you're here, or Doctor Götze?" Zimmerli asked.

"No!" Sonder replied. "Doctor Thalmann. No one else."

It was Thalmann who had called him in for an examination when his cough had persisted. And it was Thalmann who, a few days later, had told him to prepare himself for further tests. Anyone who had worked in a clinic for years knew the significance of further tests, of the possibility of a biopsy. And his premonition that this could be the beginning, the beginning of the end, had never been refuted up to now. It had been Thalmann who had changed Sonder's mind when he wanted to refuse an operation. Of course the situation was serious, no one needed to tell him that, an operation might even save his life. But at what cost? The fear of being dependent, at the mercy of people and machines, gnawed at him. An operation, he feared, could easily be the first step toward that. Once in a hospital bed, you lost the possibility of determining the further course of events yourself, and when to stop.

Thalmann had meant well, of course, when in lengthy conversations he had urged him to be reasonable, to agree to the operation. And Sonder had let himself be talked into it. Whether that was reasonable in the end was still an open question.

"Herr Sonder," Bruno Thalmann called from the door. "How good to have you here again!"

Sonder smiled when he saw the doctor rushing toward him, and stretched out his hand. He gazed into the pale, beardless face that still looked quite young and enthusiastic, that along with his slight body radiated boyishness, innocence. But the rimless glasses and the white coat buttoned in the back corrected that impression. They suited the image of a serious, sensitive doctor.

"Good day, Herr Thalmann." The strong handshake of this delicate person was always a surprise to him; Sonder liked it. "Fine," he said in answer to the question about his health. "I should be satisfied, they tell me."

"You look well," Thalmann said. "And the weather was splendid, wasn't it." Thalmann meant what he said. Sonder really did look good, much too robust for retirement. To Thalmann's mind, they could still expect things of the small, somewhat stocky man with the shaggy moustache and the dark hair streaked with gray, unruly despite its short cut. But his eyes didn't have the same spark as before—they looked dull, almost sad.

"Yes, yes. I now know every hill there, every bit of woods. It was good to be alone from time to time." Sonder spoke slowly, without emotion. His smile wasn't convincing, nor was it meant to be. He knew that he couldn't fool Thalmann, at least not for long.

"Do you have any traces of pain?"

"It's not the pain. I can live with that."

"What is it, then?"

"The uncertainty," Sonder said after a brief pause, "that's the worst. The uncertainty about how it will go and . . . the disappointment." His voice faded; the last words came out in a whisper.

"But Herr Sonder, I've told you that you're not bad off." Thalmann said this forcefully, as if scolding a child who wouldn't listen. "You know that your chances are good, better than most people's in your situation. I've explained that to you. It's important, most important that you . . ."

Zimmerli walked through the open door. "Please excuse me, I need something from my . . ."

"Yes, yes, come in." Thalmann noticed only now that Zimmerli had taken over Sonder's locker, and he quickly motioned to Sonder to follow him.

They had just reached his office, Thalmann's hand was already on the door handle, when Professor Bäni rounded the corner, followed by Doctor Götze, his body bent forward and his arms churning, trying to keep pace with his superior. The two pathologists always had a certain comic air when they appeared together, because of their dissimilarities. Professor Harald Bäni, known since his student days as "Caesar," was a tall man, six-feet two at least, and still slender at sixty, a fact he pointed out proudly. His angular features were striking, no doubt about it, and gave him a dignified air. Beside him Horst Götze, with his short, round shape and his lack of self-control—not only in his movements—seemed rather childlike. He gave the impression of not having quite matured.

"You don't mean you're coming back to work!" Professor Bäni, shaking his head, held out his hand to Sonder. "Why aren't you resting and enjoying life? Or are you already tired of doing nothing?"

Sonder struggled for a reply. He had retired—Caesar was letting him know that. Retired in every respect.

"If you insist, we'll find some light work for you," Bäni continued. "We had to find a replacement for you, of course, you can understand that, and Herr Zimmerli is hardworking and will remain with us. We didn't think you would return to work so close to retirement. But naturally I'm happy that you're doing so well. We'll find you some light work, as I said. You can understand that." Then Bäni nodded to Thalmann in what looked like an order to take care of Sonder.

"Yes, of course," Sonder murmured, having also shaken the soft, damp hand of the assistant medical director.

"My goodness," Doctor Götze began, pointing to Sonder's chest, "you really got a warning shot that time, eh?"

"More than a warning shot," Sonder growled.

Götze ignored the remark. "Don't take it too tragically. We have capable doctors here, you know."

The two figures were suddenly enveloped in a blaze of red, their voices far away. Sonder felt paralyzed, frozen. A hand gripped his arm tightly; he knew that it was Thalmann's and he let himself be led away compliantly.

There were two desks in the room. Thalmann's was to the left against the wall, and to the right, placed slightly at an angle to allow a view through the window, was that of Pat Wyss. She was writing her dissertation and worked here part-time, mostly in the afternoons. Bruno Thalmann pushed the chair next to his desk a little forward, cleared it of a pile of medical journals, and indicated to Sonder to take a seat. Then he rolled his chair closer and sat directly across from Sonder, so close that he could grip his arms.

Sonder hung more than sat in the chair. He couldn't focus his eyes; he looked right through the doctor, through the wall behind him as well, through all the walls of the clinic. He looked out across the lake and the mountains, across countries and continents and out into space, rushing toward infinity. And his thoughts moved at the same speed, without cease. Nor would they mirror any-

thing, Sonder felt, once they had caught their own reflection at the edge of infinity.

Sonder didn't know how long Thalmann had been
speaking to him, what fraction of eternity he had taken
trying to convince him of something or other, before a
strong shake of his arm that must have taken all of Thalmann's strength brought him back to the clinic, back to
Thalmann, but back as well to Bäni and Götze. Thalmann was speaking intensely, his voice muted, as if he
were planning a conspiracy.

"Forget those two out there," he said, "they don't
count; they're totally unimportant to you. You must believe in yourself and not listen to their . . . stupid prattle.
What do they know, anyway?"

Sonder had never heard the doctor speak like this.
Thalmann had never expressed any doubt about his loy-
alty to his superiors, in word or gesture.

"You must take up the challenge," he continued,
meaning Sonder's illness, which Sonder at first did not
comprehend. "You must defend yourself. It's your only
chance. Just don't give up the fight prematurely . . ."

Struggle, battle, fight. He was always hearing these
words, it occurred to Sonder, as Thalmann continued
talking. It seemed as if it all depended on battle, as if
without it he could write off everything. And "everything"
to him meant his future, the one he had just recently
written off anyway. So he was to fight, was he! But how?
What did Thalmann mean by that? What did he understand of battle, he of all people, fragile as he was? He
was much too proper to be able to win a battle. He
couldn't even give orders—no, he requested those who
worked under him to do this or that. But as a doctor he
was suddenly demanding, demanding that Sonder take
up the fight. A nice man, serious too, it was certain he

meant well. But how was Sonder to imagine a polite battle?

After a few moments of silence, as Thalmann was beginning to fear he was talking to a blank wall, Sonder suddenly asked: "Fight! What do you mean? Do you mean like a bullfight?"

His voice was clear; he appeared to be in total control of himself again. His expression was expectant, his eyes held a trace of defiance. Was it a trap? "If you wish, a bullfight," Thalmann felt obliged to reply. And he knew as soon as he had spoken that this was the right answer.

A sympathetic smile crossed Sonder's face, sadly triumphant. "For the enjoyment of the spectators, but without any chance whatsoever."

Thalmann stood up and walked slowly over to his desk, leaning on it and looking briefly at the ceiling. "You're making it hard on yourself, Herr Sonder. Why do you want to . . ."

"Have you ever been to a bullfight?" Sonder wasn't willing to drop the subject.

"No, nor will I ever go to one." And Thalmann was relieved to see Sonder's expression brighten.

"But you should, really. And then go to a slaughter-house afterward."

"A slaughterhouse?" Thalmann shook his head in confusion. "Why would I do that?"

"To a slaughterhouse, yes. You know that I was a butcher once. That's the profession I was trained for, butcher."

"You mentioned it once." Thalmann could not imagine where this conversation was leading.

"When I first came to Zurich, I worked in a slaughterhouse. I stayed for three months, not a day longer."

"Was the work so hard?"

11

"I was strong then. No, it was something else."

"Yes?"

"The animals there are led into a huge hall, prodded in, mostly. One animal after another. Then they stand there, stock still, paralyzed by the smell of warm blood and the rattling of the chains. And they have to watch as the animals in front of them are killed, watch them collapse—but they don't react. They don't defend themselves. They can't defend themselves. They don't know how."

There is no appropriate behavior for mass murder, went through Thalmann's head. Apparently this was true of animals as well.

"It seems as if they're simply waiting for the bolt gun, as if it would be a relief." Sonder then described his work there, how he stood on a grating and cut out the organs, always the same, one animal after another, day after day. Assembly line work, as he put it, unworthy of either man or animal. Then he compared the slaughterhouse to his own butcher shop, the one he had bought. It was different there, he said. There he had taken care to leave the animals their dignity.

Thalmann, who had sat down again in the meantime, considered why Sonder was telling him this, and considered also asking him why he had given up his own business, but then decided against it. It didn't seem important. From the hallway he could hear the high, penetrating voice of Imelda Stäuble, the executive secretary.

"Slaughterhouse or battle?" Sonder asked after a while. "What do you think, which is more fair to the bull?"

"But you yourself said that the bull doesn't have a chance!"

"Yes, but that's unimportant, the fact that he doesn't have a chance. The spectators know that, but the bull doesn't. And what the bull knows is what counts. I doubt that it is his life he is fighting for, or that he really feels he is a victim. When you look at him, it's more like he feels he is the incarnation of life itself. He is the one who attacks, who seeks the fight, without fear."

"Well, the bull doesn't have any other choice," Thalmann interjected, "he simply has to fight. He's provoked into it."

"You think he has to fight? I tell you that he is *allowed* to fight. As opposed to the slaughterhouse. There he sees death, but is helpless because he can't identify the enemy. In the arena, he knows who his enemy is. He's allowed to fight, and that's what he's made for."

It was clear to Thalmann now that Sonder was talking about something that concerned himself. But it wasn't like him simply to go on like this. What was the man trying to say? Where was he headed? The thought that Sonder could be comparing his fate to that of an animal seemed so outrageous that he rejected it immediately. "I don't understand what you're getting at."

"I envy the bull. I envy him his toreador, and the cape used to provoke him." There was a beseeching tone in his voice as he sat there with his hands outstretched, palms up.

Thalmann was confused. He no longer understood Sonder, whom he had always thought of as reasonable, sensible, and not unintelligent. But now—since the onset of his illness, really—he was implacable, he didn't want to understand what it was all about. "It's another fight I'm talking about. You know that! I'm talking about you."

"Then tell me how you fight against your own body, your own body that's betraying you?"

13

"The main thing is your attitude toward your illness, toward death as well, if it comes to that. The fight I'm talking about . . ."

"I'm not afraid of death," Sonder interrupted him vehemently, "unless it's a death like in this clinic." He stood up, took a few steps to the window, and looked out at the woods close by. "I've seen enough. I know what happens to people here. I don't wish to be treated, to waste away, like that. In earlier times soldiers went back to the battlefield to deliver the coup de grâce to the critically injured. There is no grâce today. Once medicine has you in its claws you're delivered up to what is called progress. And everything is sacrificed to it, even human dignity. In the end you're lying in some sterile room with a cross on the wall, and the machines you're hooked up to have replaced your will to live and appropriated your fight against death. You aren't alive then, you're vegetating; you've become a number in some statistic, nothing more."

Thalmann felt helpless. He wanted the best for each of his patients, and was convinced that he was acting accordingly now. But Sonder seemed to him like a plaintiff who is accusing his lawyer—himself, that was to say—of entering a plea for torture instead of death. There was no point in trying to have a reasonable conversation with Sonder today. There was no approach he could take, no argument he could make that would lead to a positive outcome. What was there left to say? In the face of the old man's contrary attitude, his encouragement seemed meaningless. Nevertheless! "You shouldn't torment yourself with such thoughts. You'll ruin the time you have left, all the years you can enjoy without infirmity. When it reaches that point, each of us must take what comes."

"But you can help it along a little."

14

"What! You can't mean that!" The man continued to astonish Thalmann. He wouldn't have expected this of him, no—of Sonder least of all.

Leaning with his back against the window, Sonder looked into the somber face with its two vertical lines between the eyebrows, the lips pressed together. "We had a dog at home. One day, after the dog became old and sick, my father put on his hunting clothes. It wasn't hunting season. Then he took his rifle and went out with the dog. You wouldn't believe how Bello, that was the dog's name, acted. He was transformed. It was as if all of his ailments had disappeared. Not far from our courtyard my father set him on a trail. I was amazed. He ran off with his tail wagging, his nose to the ground. For a few minutes he came to life. It was an unexpected moment of happiness. Then, when he stopped after a few yards and looked back, panting hard, a shot rang out. I wept with anger. My father didn't say one word for the rest of the day. He locked himself in his room and drank. Today I can only respect him for what he did. But as a human you can't expect that much understanding from another human."

So it was as Thalmann feared. Sonder really was comparing his fate to that of an animal, he thought with horror. As if there were no God and no eternity, he was comparing the worth of his life to that of an animal. "So you've already considered suicide?" Everything must now be done to get Sonder into the appropriate therapy.

"No, something more like an accident," Sonder said quietly.

"I don't understand."

"I've thought about going up into the mountains, to experience the happiness I once felt there. I could climb up until I couldn't go any farther, neither forward nor backward. They say that freezing to death is pleasant. You simply dream your way across."

"You don't mean you could feel happy doing that, knowing what was to come," Thalmann cried out in bewilderment.

"Yes. Like our dog. He knew very well that it wasn't hunting season."

2

Pat Wyss ordered a steak with morel mushrooms, passing up the noodles, and Professor Bäni decided on the rognon de veau à la moutarde. While the professor studied the wine list, Pat looked around her, amused by the waiter's red-and-black livery uniform. She didn't like uniforms and found this one laughable. It quickly became clear to her that Caesar was a regular here—they addressed him as "Professor." And he was shown immediately to a little table in a rear alcove that indeed was reserved for him. He must dine here often, she thought, probably with his secretary.

"Would you like a Burgundy? It would go well with the morels," Bäni said without looking up from the wine list.

"Fine." Sitting to one side of him, Pat studied his face, the slightly receding forehead that ended in the hint of a Roman nose, his square chin, and the scar down the left cheek that extended to the corner of his mouth. Not for the first time, she felt that his tanned face contrasted artificially with the snow-white of his hair. A picture of the Arc de Triomphe hung over his head.

After Bäni had ordered a Chambolle-Musigny 1976 he smiled at Pat in self-contentment, and his two gold teeth gleamed, souvenirs, along with the scar, of a test of courage from his student days. "And how is your work coming along? Are you making progress?" Bäni was referring to the dissertation that would promote Pat Wyss to a doctor of medicine. She was analyzing the metastases of lung tumors being treated by chemotherapy.

"Yes, yes, it's taking shape." Pat liked to leave her superior a bit in the dark as to how far along she was with her work; he wasn't a great help to her in any case. She calculated that she would be able to give him the first, and probably final, version of it in a few weeks. She had been told by colleagues that he would only correct her punctuation and perhaps rearrange a sentence or two, nothing more.

"Good. By the way, if you wish you can come along to Stockholm. I'll find the funds for it, somehow."

Pat was puzzled. Then she remembered that the Conference of European Pneumologists was meeting in Stockholm that fall. Caesar was planning to present selections of her work there. He had alluded to this before. She thought of Imelda Stäuble, who often accompanied Caesar to conferences.

"Perhaps you'd like to present your findings yourself?" Bäni asked, as if he knew the answer. "That's up to you, of course."

"No, I'd rather not!" Pat quickly rejected the idea.

Why was Caesar making this offer, she pondered. What did he expect from it? Was it supposed to be simply an incentive for her to finish her work, or did he imagine her role as that of companion? Caesar enjoyed being seen in the company of young women, a fact hard to ignore. Was that his motive? If he merely intended to draw the attention of several of his older associates to himself by parading a young female colleague at his side, she did not have any great objections. But how could she be sure that was all he intended?

"Have you ever been to Stockholm?"

"No, not yet."

"There is always enough time at conferences to have a look around at other things as well," Bäni said patronizingly. "As a rule, not much of anything new is presented at these things. I have to be there, of course, it's expected of me. On top of which, I'm serving as chairman of one division. And don't forget that a conference is the ideal place to advance oneself. One can often make connections beneficial to one's career."

Had Caesar actually winked as he had said this? Pat wasn't sure whether she had imagined it or not. He had smiled, in any case. Did he expect her to take Imelda Stäuble's place? She was dying to ask, but that would clearly be going too far. Everyone at the clinic knew of the relationship between those two, that was true, they had made no effort to hide it; but mentioning it had its price, that was known as well. Bruno Thalmann's predecessor, it was said, had been fired for making precisely this suggestion in a drunken moment at the annual Christmas party. Caesar had not found it amusing.

"So. Can I count on your participation?"

"Yes, of course! Gladly." Why should she object to an all-expenses-paid trip to Stockholm. And she wasn't defenseless, after all. Nevertheless, she hoped that the secretary, whom she considered a boring clotheshorse, would come along as well. Her presence could save potential embarrassment. Pat hated Caesar's casual touches, his caresses under the mantle of fatherliness. In Stäuble's presence they ceased.

"Agreed, then," the professor said. "I'll see to it that

you're registered. The financial part, as I said, will be taken care of."

Pat nodded. Her feelings for Caesar had changed considerably in the months she had worked with him. As a student, impressed by his magnificent lectures, she had thought of him as a great personality, but he had lost some of this greatness since then. Her enthusiasm had waned not only because of his relationship with his secretary; his conservative views had disappointed her as well. Behind the brilliant lecturer she had expected to find a free spirit, a progressive mind. It now seemed to her that his lectures were brimming with platitudes designed to ingratiate himself to his students. The fact that she remained indifferent to him—didn't reject him—was due in part to his previous performance as a teacher, but also in large part to Götze, who bore the brunt of all of her hostile feelings toward disagreeable superiors. And Caesar had always taken her side in her sometimes stormy arguments with the assistant director.

Bäni took the glass the waiter handed him, stuck his nose in it briefly, and drank from it noisily. He then stared at the ceiling long enough to make the waiter nervous before placing the glass on the table. "It's fine," he said then, and as the waiter gratefully filled his glass, he added, "It could be a degree or two warmer, but that will take care of itself."

Pat assumed that he had made this comment for her benefit alone. He couldn't pass up any opportunity to demonstrate or allude to his expertise on almost any subject.

"Cheers, Patrizia."

Pat didn't mind Caesar calling her by her first name, but it did bother her that, with the exception of two elderly aunts, he was the only one who used the name Patrizia.

She had once told him, alluding to ancient Rome, that the time of the caesars was past, and that she preferred to be called Pat. She found inappropriate, at least for herself, a first name that directly expressed the domination of father and forefather. In her opinion, mother and foremother were just as important, probably even more so. Bäni had reacted to this waggish, if essentially serious, comment by referring to her ever since by her baptized name, Patrizia.

"Salve, Caesar," slipped out of her. For a moment she was startled by her boldness and felt her face turn red. But the professor's hearty laughter alleviated her fears. He loved his nickname, after all, and she knew too that he was well disposed toward her. When he had asked her during her exams if she would like him to supervise her dissertation, she had been flattered by the offer. In the interim it had become clear to her that he was well disposed toward all his exceptional female students. They clearly had an easier time with him, which Caesar would never have admitted, of course. He simply referred to attractive students as intelligent, which was also a basis for his test grades. Pat was still unsure whether this evaluation was merely a trick, or whether he actually believed that good-looking people were smarter. But it was true that he was convinced that tall people were superior to others. Now and then he ridiculed quite openly his assistant director's short stature.

3

After the meal, the Chambolle-Musigny, and the unexpected invitation to attend the conference, it wasn't easy for Pat to concentrate on her work. She read the reports that had piled up on her desk and occasionally took notes on one of many pieces of paper lying around, or made tables of numbers and letters. Now and then she balled up a piece of paper and tossed it toward the waste basket standing almost ten feet away. She hit it often; obviously she had had practice. A long-stemmed rose towered over the seeming disorder—she bought one each morning to bring a little touch of color to the grim stacks of files. To the right, on a small table, stood a microscope surrounded by cartons of histological slides. From time to time she rolled her chair over, pushed her reading glasses up on her head, and looked into the microscope. She made a serious impression at work and was serious in her intentions, despite her conviction that minor mistakes were insignificant and would never be noticed. She even sometimes doubted the significance of her efforts.

Pat was seated at the microscope when someone knocked at the door, but she paid no attention, assuming it was someone looking for Thalmann who would leave on seeing he wasn't there. But when the door didn't squeak shut as usual, she turned around and saw a familiar figure she couldn't quite identify through the frosted glass of the door, the head inclined slightly forward, an ear to the pane. "Yes," she called now, loudly, "come in!" She rolled forward in her chair, then leaped up and hurried to the door. "Hello, Herr Sonder, how are you?" she called happily as a tousled head appeared in the opening.

Gottfried Sonder, confused by her enthusiastic greeting, hesitated a moment before he took her hand. "Good day, Fräulein Wyss, yes . . . actually, I wanted to . . ." But he was not at all disappointed to have found her there alone. He liked the "lady doctor," as he often called the restless young woman; he particularly liked the expressive play of her large, dark eyes.

"But come in! You can wait for Bruno here." Pat didn't mention that Thalmann was at a meeting and wouldn't return for some time. She knew what had transpired that morning. Thalmann had told her about Sonder, about his strange behavior—as her colleague called it—and of the unfortunate encounter with Caesar and Götze. Thalmann had asked her to find a little time for Sonder, if the occasion arose.

"I don't wish to disturb you. You must have a great deal to do."

"You're not disturbing me, Herr Sonder. Come in, sit down." Pat adjusted Thalmann's chair for him. Then she bent down quickly to clean up a pile of papers that hadn't made it to the basket.

"How about a cognac?" she asked, taking her seat.

"Why not? Since it's forbidden, during working hours."

"Then I'll allow it now." With a quick gesture she

produced a bottle of Hennessy and two snifters from a desk drawer, poured, and handed Sonder a glass. "To your last month with us, and to the time thereafter, of course."

Sonder avoided the thought of the future; he wanted to be able to enjoy these moments with Pat in peace. It had been a long time since anyone had offered him a cognac. Nipping at his glass, he tried to remember when the last time had been.

Pat placed her empty glass on the desk. "I have to down it in one gulp," she explained, laughing, as she saw Sonder's astonished face.

"Well," Sonder said, and took an even bigger gulp, still searching his memory. And then he recalled that he had last drunk cognac at Fritz Lütolf's funeral. Lütolf had suffered from lung cancer, had been a heavy smoker.

"You surely have another trip planned. Where will you go this time?"

"I don't yet know," Sonder answered, desperate for a way to change the conversation. If he asked about her dissertation she would undoubtedly mention lung cancer, might even say how many cases she had already evaluated. Cases! Pathology truly wasn't a good place for a sick person.

"But you do have plans?" Pat asked obstinately. His future, his plans, must be discussed. How else could she encourage him?

There was no escaping it. Sonder felt backed into a corner. Not by Pat—she would be the last person he would criticize. It was his problem alone, he knew that. His thinking had been poisoned by his illness. There was no other subject for him anymore. "I have to deal with this thing first," he said softly, and rapped himself hard on his breastbone with the knuckles of his right hand.

That was the reason he was here, after all, it occurred to him. He had wanted to ask Doctor Thalmann a favor. Why not the lady doctor? he asked himself now—yes, why not her? "Would you do me a small favor?" And at that moment Sonder had the feeling that if he could expect help from anyone, it would be from her.

"But of course! What is it?"

"Could I perhaps see the nodule they took out of me?" And watching the doctor anxiously, he nodded in the direction of the microscope, its light still on.

Pat hesitated, wondering what he hoped to learn from this. Sonder could not possibly recognize what he would see; it would therefore be impossible for him to verify the diagnosis. So what was the meaning of it? She could tell him anything she wanted. Could. But she knew that she could not lie to him.

"So? Will you show it to me?"

"I don't know if I'm permitted to." Pat caught herself looking for a way to gain time. But she quickly saw that she had no choice but to give in. To refuse his strange request would only disconcert him still more.

"You weren't worried about regulations when it came to the cognac, were you? It could be important to me," he added, as Pat looked at him thoughtfully.

"Fine, I'll get the slides. There's nothing to hide, after all. Wait just a moment."

Sonder leaned back in his chair as Pat left the office, and studied the landscape photographs over Thalmann's desk. Two in fog, one against the light. Then he looked at the opposite wall, where five pictures from a commercial calendar were hanging, their colors ornately bright. There was something unusual, mysterious about these captured images. They could have been microscopic exposures, Sonder thought. What if his growth looked like that, what then? He had seen countless such nodes, in lungs as well, in men and women, old and young people. But he had never seen his own. Perhaps he should have an image of what was threatening him, he had thought after his conversation with Doctor Thalmann. Perhaps he should have an image—something concrete—of the thing that had troubled him all these weeks. Who knew, perhaps then he would be able to deal with his illness in some way he wasn't yet familiar with, perhaps even take up the battle demanded of him. Perhaps. At least he could get some image from the microscope, unfamiliar as the instrument was to him.

"Here's the corpus delicti!" Pat shook the cardboard file in her hand so that the glass gently tinkled. They both smiled. Sonder, because it was impossible for Pat to hide her concern.

He drained the rest of his cognac, rose slowly, and walked over to the microscope, where Pat had opened the file. He watched as she chose one of the colored slides and laid it on the microscope stage. It passed through his mind that this was a part of himself, sliced thinly and numbered, a part of himself that had made itself autonomous. And it was this knowledge, that it was his own flesh that had turned against him, that kept him from being able to deal with his illness. He didn't want to think about the fact that the cancer was a diabolical outgrowth of himself, growing in his body as self-sufficiently as a parasite, spreading, suddenly appearing in other organs to destroy in the end the body that was its own life support. It was an idea his mind couldn't accommodate, he could find no logic in it. How do you fight against something that is without logic? A broken limb, pneumonia, a heart attack, all these he could understand, or gallstones or diabetes or syphilis. But to him there had always been something unnatural about cancer, something dark, perverse.

After she had focused the lens for him, Pat placed Sonder's right hand on the adjustment knob. When she took his hand she felt resistance at first, then, as the hand relented, a slight trembling. Agitation or fear? She was sure that she had never seen this strong hand shake before.

Sonder looked into the microscope, intent but restrained. For a while he merely looked, then he began to turn the knob, shifting the slide in all directions, slowly at first, then faster. He watched spellbound as the image constantly changed, as the forms of the specimen mutated and yet repeated themselves continually. Pat explained to him that the red garlands were cancer cells and the green color was mucus. Sonder soon had to admit to himself that no, it wasn't frightening. Strange, yes, but not frightening. Actually, it had an exotic beauty. Yes, if he were objective, if he weren't looking at something he knew was so evil, he would have to confess that the colorful patterns had a certain beauty. Could one not speak of beauty when referring to a poisonous snake, he thought, just because it was dangerous or had struck?

Sonder leaned back and passed his hand over his cold, damp forehead. "And if something like this shows up somewhere else, in the bone, for example, does it look like this as well?" he asked, concealing the slight dizziness he felt from the shifting movements of the slide.

"It could," Pat answered. "But why speak of that, Herr Sonder? Nothing showed up during the examination that . . ."

"They told me I had to be examined periodically, every three months," Sonder interrupted. "They scarcely would have told me that for no reason."

A good argument. "That is a precautionary measure. It's the same for everyone who has a lung tumor. Or rather, had." She was aware of how weak her words sounded. But what else could she say?

"But you can ascertain how much of a threat it is. You do that kind of thing here every day."

It rankled Pat that she couldn't withstand Sonder's sharp gaze; she felt that he could see right through her evasions. And she wanted to be honest with him. "Yes, that's true, but not so precisely." And was not surprised when Sonder asked for the report on the findings and prognosis, straightforwardly, without any sign of self-pity. He wanted the whole truth, a sober, scientific analysis of his tumor. The imprecise answers and vaguely encouraging words must exasperate him. He had seen too much, he knew too much even to halfway imagine that he was safe. Perhaps only the total truth would be of help to him. But there was no such thing. Not concerning what he was interested in, his prognosis.

As Pat studied the report, Sonder looked into the microscope once more, virtually diving into his innermost self. And like a leap into a blue-gray body of water, under the surface of which one finds oneself in a totally new and dangerous world, Sonder found himself in his own inner world, one that fascinated him despite its threat. But the unreal forms and colors that he had never seen in his own world unconsciously made him doubt that this really was a piece of himself. He began to gain some distance on what was called "tumor" or "cancer"; he no longer viewed what he was looking at as something that had originated in him, he saw it much more as something that had been planted in him, whose origin must lie outside his body.

Pat jumped at the sound of loud knocking. Doctor

Götze entered the room, a cigarette in the corner of his mouth, a book clamped under his arm. "I only wanted to say that I won't be there tomorrow night until after eight. I have another appointment." He stood there imposingly, sure of himself. And why not? He was a university instructor, after all, with a good chance for a full professorship.

"The meal is scheduled for eight!" What more could she say? Götze had let her know how important his presence was at these occasions. If the chief insists, he had said. Götze! His appearance might inspire laughter, but his presence produced loathing. To Pat he was like an embryonic monster, egocentric, undifferentiated, incapable of pleasure. He was plump, with a large head and a smooth-shaven face dominated by oversized horn-rimmed glasses, which appeared to be supported more by the indentation between temple and cheekbone than by his small nose. And the thick lenses he needed for his poor eyesight magnified his eyes and gave him a threatening and sometimes startled expression.

Only as Götze turned to go did he apparently notice that Sonder was seated at the microscope. "What the devil are you doing there? Are you planning to take up histology?"

"I was only looking at my lung." Sonder said this quietly, almost coolly. But Pat felt the delicate vibrations he was giving off, and knew that he was raging inside. He seemed like a volcano to her, one that only appeared dormant. A person needed fine instincts to recognize the threat of an eruption.

"What is it you're looking at?" Götze hissed, and turned to Pat. "This won't do. What were you thinking of? You can't do this! It's confidential!" Götze's voice swelled to a scream, and ashes from the cigarette hanging

29

from his mouth fell to the floor. "Have you lost your senses?"

"It's his lung, after all. A patient gets to see his own X-rays," Pat said, apparently equally cool. But her eyes were beginning to flicker dangerously.

"This is unbelievable," Götze snapped, retreating. He must have realized that he couldn't win against her. Twice already after a rude confrontation Bäni had taken her side—once she had been so angry that she had sworn at him. He slammed the door so hard the glass rattled.

"I could kill that man," Sonder growled, somewhat louder than he had intended.

"That would be an act of charity, Herr Sonder, an act of charity on behalf of all of mankind." The look that Pat directed at the door could not have been more withering and could have been matched only by an obscene gesture. "And this idiot is going to be a professor."

"Caesar's successor, perhaps?"

"No, he applied for a position at the university and is supposedly on the short list. Simply ridiculous!"

Sonder shook his head.

"When it comes to humanity, the people who make it do so through a process of negative selection." Pat could get really worked up on the subject. The higher someone's place in the hierarchy, the more suspect he was to her, she said. That was true of every position of power, whether in politics or the church, the army or science. The drive for power was an instinct, and where instinct prevailed there was no room for humanity. Every system faltered on this principle, for man was not wise, no matter how much he deceived himself with his "homo sapiens." Perhaps man really was only an animal, Pat continued her thought, who, thanks to the combination of upright posture and opposable thumbs, totally by accident had strengthened the cerebral cortex. But the cerebrum, apparently responsible for all progress, failed in all important decision-making because it was controlled by the archaic, primitive brain that humans had carried with them unchanged from their animal past. "Imagine, Herr Sonder, man has the knowledge to feed all of humanity and therefore the means to save the earth, but he won't apply this knowledge. The primitive brain of this power-hungry, egoistic creature won't allow it."

Sonder nodded. What could he say to that?

Pat was silent for a moment. She remembered why Götze had looked in. "I haven't even asked you yet. You are coming to the departmental party tomorrow, aren't you? Caesar put me in charge of organizing it."

"No, I'd rather not. You understand." Sonder didn't say that he preferred to go to a soccer match that evening. He hadn't been to a game for a long time.

"Yes, of course. But perhaps you'd have some time this weekend. We could cook something on the grill and have a talk. My parents are on vacation and I've got to take care of the house."

"Fine, that would be fine." His small, clear eyes lit up, showing that this invitation was the nicest thing that had happened to him in a long time. However, he didn't forget why he had come. "So, how does it look?" He pointed to the sheet that Pat still held in her hand.

The node had reached a critical mass, Pat said, after a brief look at the report, it was positioned peripherally —advantageous to removal—but in several places it was predisposed to intrusive growth. A bronchial carcinoma with no lymph node involvement.

"And my chances? How do they look?"

"Based on this information, roughly . . . 50 percent for the next . . . five years."

"And what does the report say?"

He had caught her, she saw it in his open, questioning face. "What it says here is incorrect, a mistake, no doubt about it. I know something about these things," she said, disturbed. "I've examined many such reports for my dissertation. You can believe me, Herr Sonder. I know all the research done in this area."

"Worse?"

As Pat was suggesting to Sonder that she go to Caesar with the slides to prove that the opinion was false, Sonder looked at the paper she had thrown angrily on her desk, and saw the large "G" written in a familiar hand.

"I believe you, Fräulein Wyss. Yes, yes, I believe you." He was busy with another thought now. Namely, whether it was a coincidence that Götze, of all people, was the one who had evaluated his tumor. Nothing positive could have come of that. Not with Götze, he was convinced.

"Anyway, the most important criterion hasn't been taken into account at all. The individual! A person's attitude has to be included in the opinion. In the end one's will to health is decisive as to how things will turn out. That means your chances are much better than described here."

"And why do you believe that?"

"Because I'm convinced that you will fight, that you won't admit defeat so easily. That's why!"

Sonder smiled indulgently. She too could not resist summoning him to battle.

His question why he had developed cancer in the first place, given her reasoning that he would have been re-

sistant to it all along, seemed logical to Pat at the time
—only hours later did she think of an appropriate
answer—and she felt he had led her into the area of
unscientific reasoning. The old man was stubborn,
prickly, didn't leave her any room to move around in—
Pat had to give him that, not without a certain respect.

"There must be a reason why the tumor formed in
me, of all people." Sonder had already put this question
to Doctor Thalmann before the operation. But his answer
hadn't satisfied him, wasn't really a response to the question he had asked.

"That's not easy to say. The most common risk factor
is cigarette smoking, but there are . . ."

"I've never smoked cigarettes. I smoked a pipe at one
time, but never cigarettes!"

"There are other causes. We just aren't too sure of
them."

"In any case, there are chain-smokers who are
healthy, and I have lung cancer. That's not logical, it's
not fair."

Pat explained that an illness would become logical
only when they had learned everything there was to learn
about it, all the internal and external factors, and that
would never be the case. And one could not demand
fairness of nature anyway, he must know that himself.
Nature wasn't concerned with the individual, its laws
applied to the whole, and it strove for balance. The laws
of existence ruled out the absolute, and therefore a society
made up of only the healthy was unthinkable. Viewed in
this light, illness itself had to be seen as something
normal.

Strange people, these physicians, Sonder thought.
They demand that you fight illness, and then when you

ask for a simple scientific explanation, they say, in effect, that nothing can be done. Or was he supposed to fight against what was normal? But beyond this contradiction, he was engrossed by a sudden thought, an idea that had occurred to him earlier, when Pat was talking to him. It seemed to him that for a fraction of a second a crack had opened, and through it he had seen something that would bring about the solution to his problem. He had to unearth this idea again. "So sick people are needed so that there can be healthy ones?" he ventured.

"Yes, in a certain sense you're right. And for the individual who is struck by disease apparently without reason, that is hard to accept, and may seem unfair."

"So according to that, I am standing in for someone who is a heavy smoker"—there was that thought again —"for a heavy smoker who stays healthy, despite three packs a day?" Sonder, looking at Pat intently, tried to remain calm and not let her see how important her answer was to him.

Pat shrugged her shoulders. "Yes," she said, "you could express it that way, if you wish." Her further comments—that he was an exception, statistically speaking, as a heavy smoker with healthy lungs was an exception—didn't interest him. He believed he had found the hook to hang his case on.

Pat was surprised when Sonder suddenly stood up and shook her hand. "Many . . . many thanks, Fräulein Wyss"—he almost said "My congratulations"—"you have been a great help to me. I don't wish to disturb you further."

"You haven't disturbed me at all," Pat said, baffled as to how she had been of help. "Come by again whenever you wish."

"Even if I don't need further help?"

"That would make me even happier. By the way, is there anything you want me to tell Bruno Thalmann for you?"

"No. It's no longer necessary."

4

It was not yet four o'clock when Sonder left the clinic. If they hadn't expected him in the first place, they wouldn't miss him now, he thought to himself. The fact that he had just missed the bus didn't bother him, he decided to walk. He didn't intend to walk far, but then he went all the way to Bellevue. From there he took the tram home, to Zone Four, between the train yard and the military barracks. He stopped at a little store near the tram station where he shopped for his basic essentials. News of his return must have made the rounds. The whole-wheat bread they always put aside for him was there as usual. He was fine, he told them, in order not to have to talk about it and to avoid the sympathy of Herr Neff—who overdid it, as did most shopkeepers. Sonder bought a sausage, some cheese, a bottle of beer, milk, and apples. That was all he required. His parsimony allowed him to save money for his travels, and even now that this justification was irrelevant, it didn't occur to him to buy expensive items. He was accustomed to simple meals.

Sonder walked the few remaining blocks to his apartment mechanically, lost in thought, until he was startled by the shrill screeching of car tires. A stream of abuse drove him back to the sidewalk. Slightly confused, he tried to order his thoughts. They concerned the idea that had developed out of his conversation with Pat Wyss, the idea that permitted him to look at his problem in a new light. His fatal illness had been meant for someone else. And Sonder didn't need to look for whom. No, he couldn't imagine anyone else it could be.

He had been at this man's mercy for five years now. There had been no opportunity for a transfer. For five years Götze had harassed him, given him assignments he could not possibly perform in time, suddenly countermanded orders he had given him, and, when Sonder contested them, accused him of insubordination. And then Götze smoked, he chain-smoked, inhaling one cigarette after another; he had often blown the smoke in Sonder's face. Intentionally, Sonder told himself. Götze must have transmitted the germ of the illness to him in this way, having robbed him first of his natural resistance. And later, when the illness broke out, when the tumor had to be removed, it was Götze who made the diagnosis, and in doing so pronounced sentence, a consciously harsh sentence. A death sentence.

Sonder imagined himself to be the victim of a cruel hoax; he felt like a fly trapped and entangled in a spider's web. And he saw the spider who was enshrouding him, inoculating him with its deadly saliva, saw how the spider was now sucking him dry, draining life from his body for itself. But it hadn't come to that yet. No, he was still alive, he could still defend himself. The fact that he had discovered this treachery didn't alter his condition, he was well aware of that, but it allowed him take up the battle. He had identified the enemy. He didn't know whether this was the battle that Thalmann and Pat had meant. Nor could anyone have told him that. What difference did it make? The important thing was for him to fight back. That meant that he could no longer remain a defenseless fly. Yes, it was now necessary for him to procure a stinger—to become a wasp—in order to attack the spider.

Sonder was fascinated at how simple everything became once he was on the path to solving the riddle of his illness. The nature of the tumor changed; he no longer saw it as his own monstrous prodigy, but as something alien that had been transmitted to him. Just as he had felt on looking into the microscope. And it was this realization that made it possible for him to defend himself, to get to the root of the evil. Even the thought that his counter-defense was coming too late to give him back his health did not bother Sonder at the moment. He had decided that he must act, he could not simply accept what had been done to him. What this demanded—namely, to render Götze harmless, even kill him if possible—did not alarm Sonder. He no longer considered the assistant director to be human, but merely a malevolent spider, an enemy.

Sonder lived on the ground floor of an apartment building built in the thirties, which had long awaited renovation. It did not bother him that this had never taken place; on the contrary, at least it had kept his rent low. He put down his bag in the corridor and went into the living room. It was filled with old-fashioned, overstuffed furniture, a small table, a bookcase, a bureau with a black-and-white television on it. The carpet was badly worn—in some places he could barely make out the pattern. In violent contrast to the modest furnishings were the weapons and trophies that covered the walls. On one wall three rifles were hanging among the yellowed skulls of chamois, with their sharp black horns, and roebuck, with their two- and three-branched antlers. To the left hung his hunting rifle, which he had never used again after his encounter with the wild boar, and to the right was his father's hunting rifle, the one he had killed the dog with, and above them, in the middle, was the carbine he had carried on border patrol. He had hung them there as other people hang portraits of their ancestors, vacation photos, amateur paintings, medals of honor, and diplomas. These things, hanging on a wall, confirmed that he had a history. The faded photograph of his wife, seated with their son standing stiffly next to her, his arms at his sides—like a soldier at attention—hung in the bedroom over his bed.

Sonder had gone into the living room to choose a weapon. A rifle, of course—what else. But now as he looked at them, the guns, each with its own memories, he hesitated. Suddenly they didn't seem right, any of them. He wasn't going hunting, after all, nor was he fighting a war; he simply wished to defend himself, to right a wrong, and a rifle didn't seem the right instrument for that. He looked at the other walls, disconcerted. There too, weapons were hanging, unusual weapons, all of exotic origin. Spears, bows with quivers filled with bright-colored arrows, two blowguns, a crossbow from Thailand, a slingshot, and a few knives and smaller utensils used in hunting. He had assembled them, collected on his journeys to various continents, and he knew exactly where each thing was from and how it was used. Here as well, every object had its history.

Sonder had begun his travels soon after he moved to Zurich, a move that had not been entirely voluntary. He had gone south at first, to Italy and Greece, then farther, to Egypt, Morocco, and Turkey. Later he had visited more exotic lands. He had been to Kenya and Tanzania, to the Amazon, to the mountains of Nepal, the jungles of Borneo, to the Galapagos Islands. Only once had he traveled with a group, and he tried to distance himself from it as often as possible. He had other interests. But above all he wished to bring nothing with him, to bear no traces of his life, he wanted to be a stranger among strangers. Only in that way could he find himself. For him, the trips were journeys into fantasy, where he could forget the realities that awaited him at home. After that he always traveled alone, often taking adventurous, sometimes dangerous paths, he was aware of that. But what did he have to lose that wasn't worth the risk?

Sonder had seen how people in other lands lived, he had spent days on end with them and joined in their celebrations, even without being able to speak their language. He observed; he knew how to do that, it was something he had learned from his father. He observed in order to understand. Words weren't necessary to understanding, he liked to say when asked. Words themselves didn't supply meaning, he said, only observation did that. "House," for example—did that mean hut, home, or temple? Did "weapon" mean life or death? And death, was it the end or a new beginning?

The weapons here on the wall were the only evidence of his travels. He had never kept a diary, and had given up photography when he noticed that it interfered with his ability to observe. He rarely spoke of his experiences, only when he was asked. His chronicles seldom met his listeners' expectations—he had a different idea of what was essential. Nor was the telling important to him. He traveled to experience, to understand, to forget—not to be able to relate thrilling anecdotes.

Sonder looked at the spears and the bows, then again at the rifles on the other wall. That day it had become clear to him against whom he had to defend himself; the only question was how. His eyes wandered from object to object in search of an appropriate implement for his task. He saw a spear flying through the air to bore into a sloth, an arrow from a crossbow piercing a bird, and he also saw a poison dart surging from a blowgun. Suddenly he took down from the wall an object he had overlooked before. It was a syringe that resembled a dart. It was a missile without a history—he had found it in the Masai steppes among the scattered bones of an antelope. He had inquired about it and learned that it was a projectile used to stun wild animals. It was used, therefore, to anesthetize, not to kill. But for this animal it had meant the end. He must have fled, Sonder assumed, and for some reason or other could not be tracked. Maybe a vehicle had broken down, who could tell. To lie paralyzed in the steppes is deadly. The vultures begin their work while the animal is still breathing. He had witnessed this cruel scene once with a dying zebra, without being allowed to interfere. It had been in a national park where they let nature take its course, where the laws of nature were protected legally from the nature of man.

Now this needle, with its bright crown of feathers, offered itself as his quill. He needed only the right implement, he thought to himself, and as his eyes passed over a blowgun he got the idea of placing the needle in a pipe and blowing it out. The thought of using his own damaged lung to send the projectile sailing through the air pleased him. He felt that in this way the fight would be a fair one, at least from his point of view. And if he could manage it, if his lung could take it, he would be over the hump, he would have overcome evil.

The leather pouch hanging next to the blowguns contained a soft brownish mass. Poison for the arrows. It had been given to him by Ricardo, his guide on the upper Orinoco River, a former guerrilla fighter and—as he said of himself—a friend to the Indians. Sonder had never believed that he would ever make use of the poison. But it now appeared to be exactly what he required for his novel weapon. He needed only to find a pipe of the right caliber. He immediately began his search, and soon carried up two pipes from the basement, but both were too big. He considered going to a plumber until he discovered that a curtain rod in the kitchen would serve his purpose. He cleaned it and sawed it into two pieces, then stuck the projectile into the longer of the two. He took a deep breath and blew into it, aiming at a pillow that lay a few yards away from him on the sofa. He doubled over at the stabbing pain in his side. I hope I haven't torn anything, he thought instantly, and at the same moment saw the needle bounce off the pillow, and this made him forget the pain, which was slowly fading. It had worked, he had hit his target from ten feet. But I'll need to practice, he told himself, even if it hurts. And the pain suddenly took on a special meaning for Sonder. As evidence of his disability, it strengthened his determination to defend himself, and further legitimated his plan.

The projectile had to be tested and cleaned and repaired, if necessary. Sonder believed himself capable of that. He would have time after his evening meal. He could certainly find the right needle at the clinic.

Sonder had placed a chair in the small garden adjoining his apartment, and when the weather was good he took his meals there. Though there was no view to speak of, at least he could see the sky. And he never forgot to take a tin bowl of milk with him for the two cats who visited occasionally. The little black one came right up at the sight of him but didn't always drink—she seemed to prefer to curl herself around his legs with her tail raised, purring, and to wind her thin, lithe body through his broad hand. The other visitor, a large tiger tomcat, approached the bowl in his own way, following an intricate path, and always giving the impression that he had come upon the bowl totally by accident. He never let Sonder out of his sight as he hastily lapped the milk, and as soon as the bowl was empty he disappeared as nonchalantly as he had come.

When Sonder walked out that day he saw the tom in the vegetable garden, lying in wait in the blackberries for a thrush. Sonder moved slowly, put down his tray carefully in order not to disturb the two, the hunter and the bird. He looked at the crouching body of the predator, stretched out, stooped, almost motionless. One front paw was suspended in air. Only the tip of his tail revealed that he was breathing. The thrush suddenly flew off, not having noticed the cat, otherwise it would have scolded him. With only a short whip of its tail, the cat sat up and began to clean itself, as if the concentration and tensed muscles of the moment before hadn't existed. Sonder didn't know whom the cat belonged to, or if he even had a home. He liked to imagine the animal as self-sufficient, spending the night here and there, and viewing the milk—and sometimes the end piece of a sausage—as a contribution toward maintaining this self-sufficiency.

5

It was Tuesday evening, shortly before seven. Traffic was unusually heavy around the train station. Flags waved in the distance, and singing could be heard. Small groups of soccer fans, dressed in blue and white or red and black separated themselves from the crowd pushing into the underground mall called Shopville. They provided unexpected patches of color in the gray confusion of the station square, which, like many other places in the city, was reserved for automobiles. The interruptions in the flow of traffic unleashed a concert of horns that only encouraged the yelling and the vehement waving of flags.

"What is all this about?" an elderly lady in the tram exclaimed, as it was briefly detained on its approach from Löwenplatz.

"It's only a soccer game," Sonder, who was sitting next to her, said reassuringly.

The woman fell silent as if she hadn't heard him, and the corners of her mouth revealed that it was a disapproving silence.

"Self-appointed banner bearers on the way to their heroes," a sonorous bass near Sonder intoned. The voice was unmistakable, as well as the thunderous roll of laughter that followed, evidence of a substantial belly. It could only be Jakob Zurbuchen, music teacher at one of the city high schools, and well-known as the columnist of a weekly paper.

Sonder looked into the fleshy, always jovial face, framed by a magnificent crown of white hair. They knew each other from Uetliberg, the men's choir that Zurbuchen conducted while bolstering the bass section with his strong voice.

"Haven't seen you for a long time, Göpf," Zurbuchen said, laying his huge paw on Sonder's shoulder.

"Hello, Jack. Yes, that's true. I've been ill."

"But you're coming back again, I hope? We could use your voice."

"All the air's been let out of me, Jack, and I'm getting ready to retire and then . . ."

"You're playing soccer these days, eh?" the music teacher grinned broadly.

"As you can see. I'm on my way there now." Sonder grasped the plastic bag with the metal pipe sticking out of it and assured himself that Zurbuchen could not have seen it, positioned as it was between his legs.

"Just see to it that there are no fatalities." Zurbuchen's laughter echoed once again through the tram before he got off at the train station.

His last remark rang in Sonder's ears. Odd, he thought, that Zurbuchen should say that. He went one stop farther, where he had to change trams, one way or the other.

Singing soccer fans got on the tram heading in the direction of the museum. Sonder looked at his watch. Ten after seven. They had enough time to get to the stadium, he calculated, even if they were going by foot. The game began at eight. He boarded the tram going in the opposite direction, along the Limmat River to Bellevue and on to Stadelhofen. There he changed to the Forch line.

Sonder was completely calm, amazingly so, he thought. He well knew that his efforts could fail, and what that would mean for him. He had taken a few precautionary measures. In his pocket he had a pair of gloves, thin ones like the kind doctors wore during an autopsy. To leave fingerprints behind would be the worst thing that could happen, especially if everything else went smoothly. But there were a few other things he had to reckon with. Götze might arrive first, or not at all. If so, there was nothing to do but give it up and wait for the next opportunity. Or he could miss his target, or the poison could have lost its power. It was even possible—a terrible thought which had not occurred to him until now—that the poison had never been potent. He had seen no reason to doubt Ricardo, and now he had no other choice than to trust the word of the jungle fighter. That too was part of the risk he was willing to take. But what if Götze didn't react to the injection? Sonder had dissolved the powder in a little water. What if it didn't bring about the expected paralysis? Would he have to carry on the battle through other means? He could use the metal pipe as a weapon! He felt a chill run down his spine. No, the use of force was out. Or he might be surprised in the act. The police would never believe that he was acting in self-defense. But even the thought of spending the rest of his life behind bars didn't unnerve him. What was the difference between a jail and a hospital? he asked himself. He would be serving time in either.

Sonder looked about him cautiously. There were only a few people in the tram, and no one appeared to take notice of him. They're going home to dinner, Sonder imagined, to sit afterward in the garden or in front of the TV, or they'll take a walk. Harmless citizens, all of them, just like himself, with their big and little problems at home and at work, financial difficulties perhaps. The usual. Sonder envied them. All of that was insignificant in the face of his problem. And it was someone else's fault—no one could have persuaded him otherwise—that he found himself in this ominous situation. He had not gone looking for battle. No, the battle had been forced upon him by Götze, who had chosen him, Gottfried Sonder. And for the nth time he asked himself why it was he who was to be sacrificed. Was it pure coincidence? Or was it like a hunt, when the hunter chose one animal from the herd? You train your sights on the superfluous one. Or the one you think is superfluous.

Sonder got off at the Forch, followed the street for a short distance and then turned off onto a field path. He knew the area from parties he had been to there, knew where the cars were parked. But he didn't take the direct route. He would make a small detour, where there was less likelihood he would be seen, to the place where he would lie in wait. He moved through the woods almost silently, crossing gullies and walking through undergrowth with a nimbleness no one would have expected of a lame old man. Sure that he had not been spotted, he reached the stack of wood in front of which the cars were parked. The first one he saw was Pat Wyss's Citroën 2 CV, adorned with cartoon figures, with Bäni's white Mercedes parked at the end. Sonder was relieved to see that the red Ford had not yet arrived. He calculated that Götze would park his car next to Caesar's, the logical place for him in every respect.

Sonder sat down on a tree stump behind a woodpile, an ideal hiding place. For one thing, he could see the

road from there, and for another, he would have Götze
within range when he parked. He had practiced with the
weapon, despite the pain it caused him each time he blew
into the pipe. He couldn't miss from fifteen feet. He drew
on his gloves carefully, as if it were part of a ritual. Then
he took out the metal pipe, with the projectile already
inside.

At two minutes to eight, Sonder was ready. He was
surrounded by silence. The cabin was too far away to
hear voices. There was an occasional rustling of leaves,
a bird or a squirrel, and from somewhere nearby he could
hear a woodpecker hammering away. Sounds that for
Sonder were part of the silence. He became strangely
agitated when he tried to imagine in detail what was to
come. It wasn't comparable to the tension he felt when
he was on the trail of a buck. There was a coldness to it
he had never felt before, a foreboding.

And suddenly he had the inexplicable sense that he
was being watched. And he knew from where. Sonder
saw the dog standing at the end of the woodpile, a dachs-
hund staring at him warily. "Get away from here," Sonder gestured with his hand. To no avail. He could hear
footsteps in the woods. He gestured again, stronger this
time. The dog didn't budge. The steps came nearer. Sonder picked up a rock and threatened the dog with it. That
was a mistake. Now the little beast began to bellow. A
woman's soft voice did nothing to stop the barking—on
the contrary, it grew louder. The voice, now quite near,
gave a command. Sonder had already gotten up by the
time the woman reached the dog. With his back to her,
he stood as if he just stepped out for a breath of fresh
air. That was sufficient.

Sonder sank back down heavily onto the stump. He
had been spotted, and at the scene of the crime. It was

precisely what he had wanted to avoid, and now it had happened. His plan to conceal the weapon and hide Götze's body here if all went well was now out of the question. Because of a little dog. The woman would be able to describe him, perhaps even to recognize him. No, he wouldn't make it so easy for them. But he couldn't accept the thought of giving up, of abandoning his plan—he simply couldn't. A setback here, now, would be nothing less than an admission of powerlessness. He couldn't afford that. Perhaps he should change his plan. But how?

A red car turned on to the road. Dust swirled. What if he carried Götze away? In his own car. Then the scene of the crime would be obscured, and no one would be looking for a little old man with a gray moustache. But how would he do it? He had not been behind the wheel of a car for nearly ten years, since he had stopped running errands for the clinic.

The car came nearer; a decision was unavoidable. Sonder shivered when he saw his adversary's features, the shivering took over his whole body. And as he stood up to take his position an invisible power held him back, pushed him down onto his seat. His limbs were leaden, he couldn't catch his breath, and his heart was pounding dangerously. Blood hammered in his head, so much so that the veins in his sweat-soaked temples threatened to burst. And he felt an odd metallic taste in his mouth.

The memory struck him like lightning, came and went. It was the same sensation he had felt when his son was missing and the neighbor's farmhand was suspected of having done something to him—he had previously been convicted of just that offense. Sonder had felt the same way then. It must be fury, righteous fury.

It required all of Sonder's strength to take a few steps

forward. The battle had begun. Ducking down, leaning on one hand, he peered through a gap in the stack of wood. The car was approaching him slowly, exactly as he had imagined. Should he really do it? Despite his reservations? The motor was turned off, Götze got out and stood by the open door, searching his pockets for something. Cigarettes, probably, Sonder thought. Götze had never seemed so vile to him, so abysmally evil in his pact with the devil. The man left him no choice. And when Götze leaned into the car to take something from the passenger seat, Sonder acted. He stood up quickly, still trembling, propped his arms on the wood and pointed the pipe at Götze. He aimed at the man's buttocks, at the blue trousers stretched tightly across them, and as he did he suddenly seemed helpless to himself, naive, with his eccentric weapon. He would have preferred a rifle now, or a pistol, something sure, at any rate. As he inhaled he was overcome with fear that he would not have the breath, the strength, to give the projectile enough power.

A sharp hissing sound, a brief whirring, and the bright circle of feathers was dangling from the blue flannel like a wilting flower. For Sonder everything froze for a moment: no movement, no sound, no feeling of hate, no pain in his chest. Only for a moment—then things came to life, slowly at first. Götze's head appeared as if in slow motion, and he grabbed behind him, in slow motion as well. Sonder ducked back down behind his hiding place and perceived everything intensely, as if he were coming out of a deep freeze. A degree at a time, the forest lit up in green, the air was filled with the shrill evening song of the birds. Sonder smelled sap and wild garlic and again felt the uncommon heat, but the pain in his chest did not return, nor the heaviness that had hindered him before

—they had been blown away. He felt only a tenseness, an almost pleasurable curiosity about the consequence of his act. He looked through the gap in the wood to observe the result of his retaliation.

Götze was staring in disbelief at the strange object he was holding up to his face, dumbfounded. "This is crazy," he gasped, before he began to yell. "Hello, who's there? Who is it?" He looked around him in distress, and yelled even louder when he couldn't see anyone. "Where are you, you god-damned idiot?" His voice broke abruptly. Then he looked briefly at the car and seemed to orient himself, deciding on the only possible direction before he headed resolutely for the woodpile.

Sonder didn't know why he stood up. He hadn't planned to. He stood before Götze, face to face.

"You, Sonder? Have you gone mad?"

"If you say so, Götze."

"What's gotten into you? You can't do this!" Götze managed to get out. His face was beet-red.

"Oh yes, I can. As you see, I can." And Sonder was astonished at how calm he was in the face of the uncertainty that engulfed the scene.

"You're sick, man!" Götze was screaming again.

"I know, mortally ill. And you passed sentence on me. Torture and death!"

"What are you talking about? You're out of you mind." Suddenly Götze remembered what was important. "What was in the syringe, tell me, what was it?"

"That's unimportant, Doctor," Sonder said, accentuating the word "doctor." "It will be painless."

"What is it? Tell me what it is." Götze was pleading with him now, in a whining voice.

"Poison. Indian poison." For an instant, Sonder thought of Ricardo. Had he been right to trust him?

"Curare!" Götze was breathing heavily. Tubocurare, pot curare, calebassen curare, went through his head, from the bark of the strychnine tree, chondodendron tomen . . . "Curare! You're trying to kill me!" His voice cracked.

"No, just rendering you harmless." Sonder was amazed that Götze didn't react to what he said. He had not understood the remark, he thought—he probably was incapable of understanding it.

The neuromuscular synapses. Curare blocked the absorption of acetylcholine. With the result that . . . Götze took one shaky step forward, he was separated from Sonder now only by the stack of wood, and made a wild grab for his adversary. Fully conscious, but paralyzed.

It seemed to Sonder as if a blind man were reaching for him, and instinctively he held out the metal pipe to Götze. "Yes, I did it with this," he said, as Götze seized the pipe. "I defended myself with my lung, Herr Götze." There was a trace of pride in Sonder's voice. "Yes, my lung. You didn't count on that."

The diaphragm lasts, breathing fails. The antidote . . . "Neostigmine, I need . . . !" A hoarse babble was all that Götze could manage.

Sonder pulled on the pipe, then pushed, noting that Götze no longer offered resistance. The poison was taking effect, incontrovertibly. Sonder wished that Ricardo, the lone warrior against evil, were here, Ricardo, whom he had been right to depend on. He would understand. He hated the exploiters.

Götze's prominent lids were becoming heavy behind his glasses. It seemed almost unreal to Sonder how they lowered, how slowly the eyes shut, eyes that had only a moment before been wide with anger and fear. There was no authority left in him, Götze could no longer abuse his privilege. He was powerless against the jungle poison, it made everyone equal. But when Götze let go of the pipe Sonder felt no triumph, no joy. Götze's collapse was satisfaction enough, nothing more, nothing less.

The body twisted. Götze fell to the left and hit his head hard against the bumper of Bäni's car. Not a pretty sound, Sonder thought, as he heard the sound of Götze's glasses breaking. Now was the time to act. Sonder immediately emerged from behind the woodpile and tried to open the trunk. Without success. He took the key ring from the car door and was looking for the right key when he heard a rhythmical whistling sound. The sound came nearer. Sonder knelt down quickly, half-covering Götze, and acted as if he were checking the back wheel of the car. A jogger ran by breathing heavily, looking straight ahead in total self-absorption. A deep sigh of relief for now.

Two spares and a large cardboard carton took up most of the Ford's trunk space. He couldn't just take them out and leave them there, Sonder decided. He feverishly sought another solution. One thing was certain. He had been seen, so Götze had to disappear, along with the Ford. Put Götze on the back seat, like a passenger! A dangerous move, Sonder thought, too risky with his driving skills. But what else could he do? Standing behind the Mercedes, with Götze's head lying between his feet, he made sure the coast was clear. Almost as an afterthought, he pressed the button to Bäni's trunk. And to his astonishment—Sonder actually jumped—it opened. The trunk was quite large and held nothing but a small crate of bottles. Why not, Sonder thought to himself, casting a glance at Götze. Let Caesar take care of his assistant director.

Sonder was accustomed to lifting heavy objects, but

this was hard work even for him. With one knee on the ground, he lifted the upper part of Götze's body onto his other knee, pressing him against the car and hoisting him slowly until he could balance his load on the edge of the trunk. Then, after one short pause for air, it took only a hard shove, one thrust, and Götze sank down into the blue-lined trunk. After he had forced his legs in, Sonder gave the man—he didn't know if he could think of him as a corpse yet or not—one last look. He could have checked, but Sonder was satisfied with a glance. He, the victim, he who had always been the victim, had rendered Götze, the perpetrator, powerless, had taken him out of the game for the moment, probably forever. His face seemed strange to him somehow; without the magnifying effect of the glasses his eyes seemed tiny.

Then, without knowing why, Sonder reached past Götze's head for one of the wine bottles. It was a Château Latour. Never in his life had he done anything illegal, had never even thought of it—so that now it didn't occur to him that he was stealing the bottle. He took it as naturally as if it were a trade. The assistant director for a bottle of wine. So much for Götze, he thought, as he slammed the lid of the trunk.

A smile crossed his face as he emptied the rest of the syringe onto the ground. He quickly went to Götze's car and laid the projectile and the metal pipe and also the bottle on the passenger seat. Before getting in, he glanced back at the scene of the crime and saw the glasses frames with the broken earpiece, the only evidence that something had taken place there. He picked up the glasses and threw them into the car. Then he got behind the wheel. It was now 8:19. After a brief search he found the ignition, and then the right key. After shifting gears a few times he was confident that everything was going according to plan. He started off jerkily at first, but then it went reasonably well, so that he was no longer afraid of attracting attention.

Sonder headed the car toward Witikon, and once there took Katzenschwanzstrasse. He wanted to avoid city traffic and planned to leave the car somewhere inconspicuous—perhaps in the parking place at the zoo—and then take the tram to the soccer game. He calculated that he would get there by the second half.

Sonder had been following a car for a few minutes before he noticed that it was a light-colored Mercedes like the one Caesar drove. The trunk! Caesar would get a real shock. Sonder suppressed the thought that he might open the trunk while still up in the woods. He didn't want to consider the possible consequences, nor did he need to, he told himself; everything had gone well thus far.

Suddenly he saw brake lights. Sonder jumped when he saw how fast he was approaching the car in front of him. His tires screeched as he slammed on the brakes, and the car skidded slightly. Sonder grasped the wheel tightly. The car simply did not want to stop. The Mercedes was right in front of him now. There was the sound of glass breaking. Finally the car stopped moving, its motor stalled. Sonder sank down into the seat, and stared at the dashboard. Any minute now someone would yank the door open furiously. The scene at the edge of the forest played in his head. He saw the bright dart sticking in Götze's buttock, saw his face, enraged, then afraid, saw Götze's body in the blue trunk. "What an idiot I am! Absolutely incapable of a thing like this."

The sound of a horn interrupted his silent lament, causing him to look up. There was no one in front of him, the car was already turning in the direction of Adlisberg. And he noticed a strange smell. It was the wine. The sound of glass had been the bottle as it broke on the floor of the car. Behind him now, a steady honking. "Thank God," Sonder murmured, as he started up the car again.

He approached the tram station at the zoo cautiously. The parking lot was to the right. He had already pressed the turn signal when it occurred to him that Caesar lived not far from here. He had done some yard work for him in earlier days. On Saturdays, particularly when trees needed to be felled. He had sawed them and split the wood for burning, earning a little money on the side. It was work he enjoyed, but he would not have done it for Caesar alone. And why should he? Caesar was concerned with his social standing even in private. He always had to be right. There was not one topic on which he respected his—Sonder's—opinion, not even when it came to hunting.

Sonder had made up his mind. He turned left. He didn't want to miss this chance to play a trick on Caesar, to cause a little confusion. Götze in the trunk and his car in front of Caesar's door! That would give the professor something to think about. Then he could show if he really always knew everything. Sonder slowly drove down Susenbergstrasse, made two turns, and parked the Ford in front of Bäni's villa. He took the plastic bag out of his pocket and placed the projectile inside. He left the pipe where it was. He didn't remove his gloves until he was walking to the tram stop, and once in the tram he rubbed the white powder from his damp, swollen hands.

6

N o, I'm sorry, he isn't here yet," said Fräulein
Stäuble. The unctuous undertone in her sharp
voice sounded unnatural, deliberately exaggerated. It intimidated the younger doctors. "No, Herr Doctor Götze
left no message."

Scarcely had the secretary replaced the receiver before Bäni appeared at the door again. He had already
inquired after his colleague several times, instructing her
to connect him with Götze should he call in. "Nothing
yet?"

"No. Rosetti was asking for him."

Bäni returned to his office in an ill humor. He had
wanted to turn over today's lecture to Götze; he felt
burned out, unable to concentrate on his manuscript, it
needed more work. One year ago at this time he had
called in sick in order not to have to deliver the unpopular
lecture on vascular diseases. Götze had taken over for
him then, and he would surely do so again, he only need
ask. But if Götze didn't show up, he would have no choice
but to deliver it himself. On arteriosclerosis, of all things,
a topic he had neglected for the last few years. It had
developed into quite a complex theme in the meantime.

It soon made the rounds in the department that Götze

was missing, as he had been the evening before. It was incomprehensible that he hadn't shown up for work without informing anyone. Even Sonder was astonished. He had assumed that Caesar, even if he hadn't opened his trunk, at least would have noticed Götze's car in front of his house. He might have overlooked the Ford in the dark, but he must have seen it that morning.

Bäni had searched Götze's office in vain for his lecture manuscript. There was no file on arteriosclerosis. Götze must have removed it. Had he predicted having, or being permitted, to deliver the lecture again? Or did he want to put one over on him? No, that wasn't like Götze, no; he could depend on him in such instances. One hundred percent. His absence without notice was therefore even more surprising. Bäni didn't think much of his assistant director. Götze had no culture, in his opinion, no understanding of music, no interest other than his career. But for his career he would do anything. Which made him a valued colleague, one who would carry out orders conscientiously. Götze himself had once referred to his efforts as "working his way up." Working his way up! In Bäni's opinion this was a euphemism for an attitude he found contemptible. It was intelligence that got one ahead, without having to work for it. He was convinced of that, and saw himself as a leading example of it.

Bäni later leafed through several textbooks looking for a summary he could use, or diagrams that would serve as the basis for his lecture. But what he found was either outdated or matched his own notes, or was confusing to him, filled with unfamiliar abbreviations. He pushed aside—not for the first time—his irritation at not having kept up with the latest research by telling himself that it was not the accuracy of what was said that was so important, but a didactically convincing presentation. But that wasn't much help either! Bäni paced his office. He chose slides from the slide carrier, almost all he could find on the subject. He could use them to gain time. And at ever-decreasing intervals he asked the secretary for news. But all he got was conjecture, and he wasn't interested in that. He was interested only in whether Götze would arrive in time to be of use to him.

He finally read through a pile of recent publications, without a great deal of confidence, hoping to find something worthwhile. He came across an article on the history of the circulatory system, hesitated, put it aside, picked it up again. Would that save him? Yes, why not digress a bit today? He could introduce the historical background of research done on the circulatory system, summarized in this article by Professor Leubi of Freiburg. The freedom to choose one's lecture material must surely fall within the sphere of academic freedom. And the students could only benefit from an interdisciplinary lecture, he thought to himself. Anyway, Bäni believed he was training more and more idiot experts, mere technicians, really, who—especially since Latin was no longer a requirement—had abandoned any manner of humanistic thinking.

He read the article hastily, underlining passages in several colors, important names in red, facts in blue, texts—primarily in Latin and French—that he found suitable to read aloud, in yellow. Bäni felt satisfied that he had salvaged the lecture; moreover, he was proud to be able to show off to his students his classically trained mind.

Before leaving, Bäni got Thalmann on the phone and requested that he accompany him to the lecture. The subject of Götze came up again during their short walk to the Department of Medicine, and they speculated further on his absence without coming up with a plausible explanation. To the students, Bäni explained that he had been forced to change the scheduled topic owing to a misunderstanding, and announced that he would give an outline of the circulation of history. There was a commotion at this, and several of the students laughed. He must be in the wrong room, one student remarked. The laughter swelled, and Bäni, having no idea what was so funny, searched for Thalmann's face in the crowd, without success. He remained in the dark until a female student in the first row took pity on him and drew his attention to his slip of the tongue. Then he joined in the laughter as well, but not very heartily; he didn't relish being laughed at. When the room got quiet again he said that too would have been an interesting topic, but he planned to speak on the history of circulation.

When Bäni began with Hippocrates, several students left the lecture hall through the back door. He proceeded to Aristotle, who had assumed that the air from the lungs went to the heart, where a mixture of air and blood was brought to a boil in the left chamber. This was the accepted view until Thomas of Aquinas refuted natural scientists with his work, *De motu cordis.* "Ridiculum igitur est dicere quod calor sit principium motus cordis," the professor quoted. With this the philosopher had shown what logic was capable of, he said with a self-satisfied smile.

More students left the room as Bäni read aloud Vesalius's discourse in Latin and translated it, like a high-school teacher. They apparently were unimpressed that the great anatomist had believed there were two vascular systems, completely independent of one another. They weren't going to be tested on it, after all, Thalmann thought, with a certain degree of understanding. It had become clear to him in the interim that Caesar was lecturing from an article that recently had appeared in the *Swiss Physicians' Journal.* He didn't understand why Caesar had asked him to come along, and it irritated him—first, because he was familiar with the article already, and second, because he had enough work waiting for him in the department.

Bäni stressed that, once again, it was a theologian who had objected to a flaw in logic, and had postulated the existence of pulmonary circulation. Then he praised the English anatomist William Harvey for his excellent study, *Exercitatio anatomica de motu cordis et sanguis in animalibus.* He called it an example of meticulous investigation and logical deduction, a formulation he had taken verbatim from his colleague Leubi. Following this, Bäni read a text in French, Descartes's reply ridiculing Harvey's work. Descartes held to the old theory of blood vaporization, based on experimentation. Further proof, Bäni commented, holding up his index finger, that there is no substitute for thought, neither observation nor experimentation. Both could be deceptive and lead to false deductions.

Some of the students who remained acknowledged their appreciation of this historical excursus with a sharp and prolonged rapping of knuckles on their desks. Even though they were few in number, Bäni basked in the applause. The acclaim of the select few was far more important than that of the broad masses.

"It's almost too hot to undertake anything serious today," Bäni said. Other than that, little was said on the way back. At the clinic they were told that Götze still had not appeared, nor was there any word from him. The general consensus, Imelda Stäuble said, was that the police must now be brought in. They at least had to inquire whether anything had been reported, an accident perhaps. Bäni himself took on this task. He became irritated the third time his call was transferred, since each time he had to start from the beginning. The man with whom he then spoke seemed to be taking notes; at least he repeated everything that Bäni told him. There was no answer at Götze's apartment in Fällanden. Götze was divorced. His wife was living with their child in the Tessin, in Lugano, as far as he knew. They didn't get along, apparently, weren't in contact with each other. A red Ford. No, he didn't know the license-plate number. Bäni grimaced at Imelda. How should he know a colleague's license-plate number?

"Nothing has been reported," the policeman said in the end. "We'll keep an eye out."

During lunch, Zimmerli told the story of a doctor who had disappeared when, following an honorary appointment, he was asked to present his credentials. He had been a phony who had never gotten a degree. Perhaps he should join in the conversation, Sonder thought to himself, offer a possible solution so that his silence wouldn't be noticed. But he couldn't think of anything other than: Götze might be down in the garage, lying in someone's trunk. So he said nothing.

7

After watering the roses, Bäni carried the deck chair out to the lawn and set it up in the shadows of the walnut tree. He wiped the sweat from his forehead with the back of his hand as he went back into the house. He poured himself a large martini at the bar and went to the kitchen for ice, where Monica, his wife, was preparing dinner. It would be ready around seven, she said; she would call him. Bäni took the paper from the table, went out again, and settled into the deck chair, protected from the evening sun, which was still beating down strongly.

He reflected on the mysterious disappearance of his assistant director, and reviewed the various hypotheses that had been mentioned during the course of the day. From time to time he reached down to the ground for his glass. Had Götze run away from something? Was he involved in fraud? Or had he simply cracked up? It happened. Suicide, perhaps? Not Götze! Or was he the victim of a crime, after all? Bäni found none of these choices pleasant, no matter what form they took. To the contrary, he was strangely titillated by the uncertainty surrounding Götze's fate. He was not the type to be ashamed of this, but he picked up the paper to divert himself nonetheless. He began reading randomly, but didn't get far. His thoughts wandered before the sentences could begin to make sense. Soon he lowered the paper again, took several sips of his martini, and stared up into the leaves. His mind turned once again to his assistant, his thoughts going in circles, becoming more and more unclear, vague. He dozed off, lulled by the monotonous clicking sound of a lawn sprinkler and by the steady sound of the water falling on dry grass. The newspaper slipped to the ground, the ice melted in his glass.

"Harald, Harald." His wife's shrill voice called from far away. Bäni instinctively felt that she wasn't calling him in to dinner. He got himself up with difficulty, knocking over his glass, and walked swaying toward the house, blinded by the bright light. "There's someone at the door!" his wife called from the kitchen. "I can't answer it!"

The bell rang again, twice. Bäni took the garden path around his sumptuous home, approaching the front door from the side, which gave him the opportunity briefly to scrutinize the man waiting there. He could not recall ever having seen him before. He was an unobtrusive man, about sixty years old, stout, bald, rather plain in his old-fashioned suit, which appeared to be a size too large for him. Nor was the face, now turned toward him, familiar. There was nothing special about him, Bäni thought, who had not noticed his clear, observant eyes, eyes that saw more than one would expect of an understanding, elderly gentleman.

"Häberli, Police Commissioner. Good evening, Professor. You phoned us today."

"What brings you here, Commissioner?" Bäni raised his eyebrows expectantly as the man extended his hand. "Do you have news of Doctor Götze?"

"We've found his car."

"Where?" Bäni quickly asked.

"Right here in front of your house," the commissioner replied quietly.

"What!" Bäni yelled. "What's that you say?"

"Your neighbor called our attention to it. It's been standing there since last night, he told us. Didn't you notice it?"

Bäni swallowed hard as he answered in the negative. The blood rushed to his head at the mere thought of being even peripherally involved in this affair. "And where is Doctor Götze?" He suppressed a derisive tone only with effort.

"We don't know. Did he visit you last evening?"

"No. We had a party yesterday, and Doctor Götze never showed up. We expected him, at the cabin. . . . His car? I was up on the Forch. What's the meaning of all this?"

Bäni nodded when Häberli asked him if he had a moment. He immediately recognized the car on the street, and didn't understand how he could have overlooked it before. The car was actually parked a few yards from the entrance to his garage. Bäni stood staring at the young man kneeling by the open door. He was removing objects from the floor of the car and carefully placing them in a plastic bag. As they walked over to him he rose with an elegant movement that betrayed athletic training.

The commissioner introduced his colleague. They nodded to one another, but the professor glanced at the youthful face of Doctor Manz only briefly. His attention was fixed on the bag in his hand. It held pieces of glass, the green glass of a bottle. The tower! The tower on the label was unmistakable. Bäni felt a chill run down his spine. The tower reminded him of the dozen bottles of Château Latour that Eugene Rusterholz had given him a week earlier, and that were still in the trunk of his car.

He had forgotten them. Twelve bottles of Château Latour '59, and he had simply forgotten them. The thought that they had been rattling around in his trunk for days gave him a shock.

"Doctor Götze seems to be a connoisseur." Manz hadn't missed the professor's interest in the contents of the plastic bag.

Bäni laughed scornfully. "Götze a connoisseur! He's totally content with dumplings, sausages, and beer." And he remembered with disgust that Götze once had found a Lynch-Bages he had been offered by mistake excellent, despite its resin taste.

"Well, a Latour '59 is nothing to sneeze at."

Bäni shuddered. The wine, the car here, and no sign of Götze! How did it all fit together? Götze with a '59! It didn't make sense. Suddenly Bäni took two steps forward—he could feel that he was moving woodenly— to lean on the car, to Manz's displeasure. Bäni bent forward and looked in, as if he were searching for something specific. He was struck by the smell of stale wine. Château Latour! Bäni struggled against nausea. "Can you make any sense of this?" he asked the commissioner dully, leaving two damp fingerprints on the body of the car.

"It's strange, to say the least," Häberli commented. "A bottle of wine and a pair of glasses on the floor, both broken, and a metal pipe on the passenger seat."

"A briefcase on the back seat and a lighter that works," Manz added.

"And Götze has disappeared," Bäni murmured to himself.

According to his neighbor's statement, Häberli said, someone must have parked the car there between five and ten P.M. Bäni was of no help. He had left home about twenty minutes to eight and hadn't seen Götze's car. But that didn't mean much. He hadn't seen the car later that night either. When the commissioner asked whether anyone at his house might know anything more, Bäni invited him in and together they went to the kitchen. His wife, however, was of no help either. She admitted having seen the car, but not to having recognized it. She had left the house the day before at four o'clock and had returned only around eleven. She had her weekly bridge game Tuesday evenings.

After searching the car for further clues, the two policemen departed. Bäni went into the sitting room and sank into an armchair. It was a room with a high stucco ceiling, costly furniture spaciously arranged, and landscapes and still-lifes hanging on the walls, nineteenth century. It could only be coincidence, Bäni reassured himself. What connection could he possibly have to Götze's Ford? The Château Latour, however, bothered him. Château Latour! This name, otherwise the source of fond memories, clawed ominously at his brain; suddenly it held an inexplicable threat. The twelve bottles in his car were a gift in exchange for a medical affidavit signed by Bäni, a professional courtesy in an awkward situation. He was well aware that a quite different opinion would also have been supportable.

When his wife called him to dinner, Bäni got up mechanically and went out to the garden where the table was set. As she served the food and poured the wine he told her briefly what had happened, but failed to mention the story about the wine. Why remind her of his forgetfulness, which had never before been this distressing? He picked at his food absent-mindedly for a while, then hastily emptied his glass and stood up. He wasn't hungry, he said, the business with Götze was bothering him.

"Why did that idiot have to park his car here, of all places?" he swore to himself as he went into the house.

Monica Bäni heard the basement door close. She had accustomed herself to her husband's moods over the years, had learned to take his escapades in stride. Some other woman would have to worry about him, had been her motto for some time now; one woman was enough, he didn't deserve more. And the fact that it was Imelda Stäuble who was doing the worrying—and she was not the first—was something she knew well from the secretary's worried calls when he left late for work now and then, or not at all.

Incredible coincidences happen, Bäni told himself on the way to the garage. One was always hearing about them. He couldn't have had anything to do with this— even the wine didn't change that, despite its vintage. And the car? Was it perhaps a sign after all, an act of revenge by Götze, who knew about the affidavit? Nonsense! A count of the bottles would prove it, Bäni assured himself. In a few moments all his doubts would be assuaged, he would find once and for all that his fears were unfounded. Anything else would be preposterous. Yet he hesitated as he stood behind his car.

Bäni slammed the lid to the trunk down with a crash, then staggered, hitting his head against the garage door. He fell, plunging into a black hole that suddenly had opened before him. It seemed bottomless. On impact he came to. He must have lost consciousness for a few seconds; he hadn't even opened the trunk yet. Or had he? The crash of the lid was still echoing. Bäni dragged himself with effort over to the stairs, his legs threatened to fold under him. He numbly lowered himself onto the steps and covered his face with his hands. Götze was dead, he was sure of it. The angle of his head left no

68

question of that at all. Bäni sat in the dark for a long
time after the timed light went out, incapable of thinking
clearly, hoping only to awaken soon from this bad dream.
After he had calmed down and grasped that nothing was
going to save him from this awkward situation, that it
was up to him alone to deal with it, Bäni stood up. He
put on the light again and paced slowly back and forth
behind the two cars.

Someone had played a bad joke on him, a macabre
joke the outcome of which was unforeseeable. That much
was certain. He really should call the police now. Surely
that was what whoever had gotten him into this also
expected him to do. And in doing so he would be at their
mercy, the commissioner's and his assistant's—he had
forgotten their names. They would return immediately
to question him, the questions would be unpleasant, they
would try to pressure him if possible. But what was worse,
he would fall into the hands of the crime reporters. And
to them nothing was sacred, everyone knew that. They
fell upon anything that promised headlines. And this
story would be exploited. They would take him apart for
something he had no control over. He would be served
up to the masses without mercy, like a piece of meat
thrown to the vultures. He, a distinguished professor of
medicine, an army colonel, and chairman of the local
church wardens as well—a man, that is, who took his
responsibilities seriously, and who had earned the full
respect of his peers. Bäni could see the headlines already:
"Dead Doctor in Trunk of Zurich Professor!" That had
to be avoided at all costs. But how? He would need help.
He thought of the names of friends in the party, of important connections, professional colleagues, weighed
their influence, their political pull. Somehow he had to
get control of this thing before they started shouting it

from the rooftops. The police were subject to the civil code, he thought to himself. Fortunately, he could count on that. But it was a sticky situation, as he was aware; it required precise planning. He decided to order the facts first, before undertaking anything.

The car had been parked in front of his house the evening before, sometime between five and ten o'clock. Bäni had learned that much from the police. He himself had last seen Götze alive shortly after six P.M., when they had left the clinic together. He had spent roughly an hour and a half at home before leaving for the party in the woods, and had not arrived home until after midnight. With Götze's car parked outside, someone must have placed his corpse in Bäni's trunk during the period he had been at home. That was only logical. But how had it happened? He always locked the garage door. He was a stickler about that. So how could anyone . . . Suddenly insecurity set in. Had he perhaps had something to do with this embarrassing situation after all? He was shaken by the thought of several incidents that still remained unclear to him. Recently he had found himself in strange situations without knowing how he had arrived there. He had dismissed these periods of amnesia as professorial absent-mindedness, told himself they were nothing more than the result of mental strain. Strain that would be relieved, he believed, when he relinquished some of his responsibilities and the burden of lecturing. Bäni stopped pacing at the horrible thought that he really might be involved in this unfortunate affair—worse still, that he himself could have . . . He had nodded off the evening before in his deck chair, he remembered, and on waking assumed that he had been asleep for an hour. Had something happened during that time, something horrible, unthinkable, that he had banished from memory? Had it come to the point where he had totally lost control of himself? He again felt the floor giving way under his feet and sank down heavily onto the stairs.

If he really had incriminated himself, had attacked Götze, then in all probability he would never know it for sure. He arrived at this conclusion after searching his memory in vain. Nor could he expect to remember anything later—this had been true of the earlier incidents as well. If he now reported his grisly find to the police, presumably he would become a suspect. They would want an alibi, and he couldn't provide one. They would ask him all kinds of questions, try to confuse him. He was afraid that he wouldn't be able to hold up under it. Not now. The police had their methods; it was common knowledge. The amiable commissioner was no threat— Bäni felt he could handle him. But he didn't trust his colleague. He could well be the ambitious type, someone who showed no regard for a person's standing and importance. And then there was the press.

It was important to take precautions now, so that things wouldn't get that far. Bäni began weighing what he knew against what the police knew. He decided that the police knew only that Götze's car was parked in front of his house, and that there was a bottle of Château Latour inside. If he got rid of the corpse now, without being noticed, and disposed of the wine as well, then Götze's car could only speak in his favor, he thought. What guilty party would want to draw attention to himself in that way? This observation supported the professor's belief that he could master any situation with his intelligence. So the die was cast, the body had to disappear. To be submerged in water, he decided, and he also quickly decided upon where—the deep pool at the bottom of the Hirschfels Falls, where the Sihl River cascaded down.

Bäni opened the trunk again, this time without shuddering. He knew what he had to do. He was used to dealing with corpses—he dealt with them in a medical capacity, after all. In this case his interest in the cause of death far exceeded his usual professional curiosity, true, but he nevertheless undertook a brief examination with total objectivity. He routinely checked the mucous membranes, palpated the bruises under the eyes with his index and middle fingers, examined the head, especially the back of the head, for further injuries. But he could find nothing more than a broken cheekbone, and this could not have been the cause of death. A fracture of the right arcus zygomaticus, he said aloud, as if dictating.

To get to the case of wine, Bäni had to grab the body under the arms and pull it toward him until the corpse rested on the edge of the trunk. He quickly established that there were no puncture wounds of the back, at least there had been no major bleeding. Then he reached over the body and lifted out the case of wine. His arms full, Bäni could only watch as Götze fell back into the trunk, his body gaining speed, and he turned away as the head hit the trunk with a metallic thud. Götze simply had no style, he thought one last time, not even as a corpse. Then he very carefully carried the wine up the steps to the basement where the firewood was stacked, and hid it behind a stack of birch wood.

Monica Bäni glanced at the clock as she heard the Mercedes drive off. It was shortly after eight. She had settled into a deck chair, puffing contentedly on a cigarillo, and watched the little clouds of smoke dissolve into the blue as Dvorak's *New World Symphony* blared from the house. She didn't ask herself what her husband had been doing in the basement for so long, nor where he was going now. She only hoped that he wouldn't ruin her evening again as he had that time in mid-April, when he had called from the airport around ten, not knowing why he was there. He had a parking slip in his pocket and the car, which it took them a long time to find, had a slight dent on the right front fender and the headlight and turn signal light were broken. They never discovered exactly what had happened that evening. Nor had they called the police. At the advice of Eugene Rusterholz, who had diagnosed overwork, her husband had gone to Flims for two weeks to rest. But his absent-mindedness had not improved.

8

Bäni drove nervously, he shifted wrong a few times, forgot to signal. But he purposely drove more slowly than usual, which wasn't easy for him. The many tickets he had received, mostly for speeding, were proof of his racing-car driving style. But he didn't want to draw attention to himself today, didn't want to be stopped by the police, today of all days. He left the autobahn at Horgen and turned in the direction of Hirzel. The lush, rocky landscape was flooded with the rays of the setting sun. Rounded hills, each crowned with one large and leafy tree, were surrounded by reed-covered moors with small ponds in between. Bäni liked this area, he had painted several pictures here earlier, when he had found the leisure to do so. His landscapes were impressive. His paintings of this area radiated sensuality, the softly curving and yet accentuated forms had something thoroughly feminine about them. Today, however, he didn't register its charm. His entire being was concentrated on getting rid of his dangerous cargo without being seen.

On the far side of Hirzel lay the wooded valley of the Sihl, already in shadow. A narrow, unpaved road led down steeply to the river, to the place Bäni had already picked out. He counted five cars—people on outings, he assumed—which would leave before it got dark. He drove a little farther and parked his car behind several medium-high bushes. From a distance he watched people enjoying themselves at the point where the river formed a quiet basin at the bottom of the waterfall. A haze hung over the water. Children were throwing stones, trying to skip them along the surface of the water.

Why here? Bäni suddenly asked himself. Why was he so certain that this was the right place? But he didn't want to spend any more time thinking about it. He had chosen the location, and once he had decided on something, he was not in the habit of changing his mind. He sat down on a bench, waiting for darkness to fall, besides which he needed some quiet. The day had been stressful for him in every respect, and there was still much to be done. He closed his eyes. From time to time his chin sank down on to his chest, and he only occasionally heard the shrill bird calls and the high-pitched cries of the children.

A sharp sizzling sound caused him to cry out, and the crash that followed knocked him from the bench. He crouched in the darkness, his arms covering his head as if to protect himself from attack. The rustling of the trees mixed with the reverberating rolls of thunder. Thoughts flashed through his head like the lightning through the darkness, briefly outlining his surroundings. But why was he here? The tree branches above him were creaking dangerously, and the trunks groaned under strong gusts of wind that appeared to be coming from all directions. And before he could move, heavy drops of rain began to fall, sweeping away the last of his dream state.

Bäni found the way back to his car only with effort, already soaking wet. Driven by the wind, the rain pelted down mercilessly, drumming on the roof like waves, drowning out even the crash of thunder. He dried his face, neck, and hands with a large handkerchief. Irritated as he was at his discomfort, he had to admit to himself that the storm had its advantages. At least he could be assured of carrying out his unpleasant task uninterrupted. His first attempt to drive down to the river ended in failure. His headlights couldn't penetrate the sheets of falling rain, and the flashes of lightning served only to silhouette his immediate surroundings. It was almost ten o'clock before the rain finally let up a bit. Bäni could see then, and set off slowly along the road. The other cars had disappeared, as he had expected. He was the only one not to have noticed the gathering storm. He knew the path that led between the trees down to the river—it was a footpath, actually, but wide enough to drive down. He lurched forward yard by yard. Branches slapped the car, then quickly disappeared in the darkness.

When he could no longer see anything in front of him, Bäni stopped and got out, he was a safe distance from the bank. He wanted to be done with the thing, the faster the better. He left his headlights on to light the way. He was surprised at how heavy the corpse was. It was unimaginable to him that he had lifted it into the trunk. It was said that people developed incredible strength under duress. He must have been under duress. He dragged the body over the soggy ground toward the river, doggedly fighting the wind and rain. Then he rested for a while, gathering his strength. He grasped Götze's body one last time and gave it a powerful shove into the roaring water. Bäni slipped and slid helplessly down the steep bank with the corpse, as nature, gone wild, threatened to swallow them both. He clung tightly to Götze in his confusion, his fingers clawing Götze's clothing. With the water up to his chest, he suddenly and unexpectedly found a hold. It was Götze's belt. Bäni's strength waned quickly as he carefully pulled himself up over Götze's body, but it lasted long enough to clamber onto the bank. He could still depend on Götze, despite everything. Bäni shook his head. Gratitude was inappropriate to the situation. He knelt down on the muddy ground in exhaustion. And really! Wasn't this situation too grotesque to be real? But even a deep sigh directed into the dark and drizzling sky, like a silent, fervent prayer, was of no help. There was no salvation, no waking up in a soft, downy bed. If only he had informed the commissioner, it occurred to Bäni at that moment, if only he had taken it upon himself to do so. Anything would have been better than this. There was no turning back now, he would be exposed as a laughingstock, and that was worse, much worse, than being a murder suspect. As a murderer one was shown a certain amount of respect, but not as a failure. Mockery and scorn was what he would get, nothing more than mockery and scorn. He didn't deserve that. He would not tolerate it.

Bäni rallied at the sole thought of getting out of there, and had already reached his car before it occurred to him that he could not simply leave the area like that. Götze had to be totally immersed in the water, had to sink into its dark depths. Each day the body remained undiscovered would be to his advantage. And he had to make use of this advantage. Bäni went back down to the water. But no matter what he did, he could neither push nor pull Götze into the river. His clothes, his belt were caught on a root. And when Bäni attempted to raise the corpse a little, he began to slip again. Not that! He wouldn't make it back up a second time. He had to accept the fact that there was nothing more to be done. And that meant leaving Götze there, certain to be discovered the next day.

"Stubborn mule," Bäni muttered hoarsely. He went back to his car and took off his muddy clothes before getting in. He rolled his shirt and pants into a ball and threw them to the floor of the passenger side, placing his shoes next to them.

On the way back he began to get a chill. It was still pouring down rain, but the lightning was receding into the distance. Bäni left the autobahn at Kilchberg. He needed help, and he knew he could expect it from Wotan, above all. He could be trusted. Wotan would be the last to leave him in the lurch.

Eugene Rusterholz's country home was built in the English style. It was situated in a large park that was landscaped only close to the house, and allowed to go wild beyond it. As Bäni turned into the drive he saw with relief that the light in the library was burning. He honked his horn a few times. He wasn't afraid of drawing anyone else's attention to himself. Wotan's figure appeared in the lighted window, darkening it before the light in the hall went on. Soon the garage door opened. Bäni drove in; there was enough space to park between the olive-green Rover and the black Jaguar.

"My God, Caesar," Rusterholz called out as Bäni climbed out of his car. "What happened to you?" He was close to assuming that his friend had suffered another "blackout."

"You cannot imagine, Wotan," Bäni sighed heavily. "A damned unpleasant situation, is all I can say."

"And where are your clothes?" For a moment Rusterholz envisioned some embarrassing sexual encounter, until Bäni pointed to his muddy clothing.

"Damned unpleasant, you won't believe it possible."

"Come on, we'll go upstairs, you can fill me in later." Rusterholz led his late-night guest into the bathroom and turned on the bath water. At his request, Bäni handed him his clothes. "It would be best anyway if you stayed overnight."

"Yes!" Bäni would have agreed to any suggestion his friend made, without reservation.

When Rusterholz returned he was carrying a pair of pajamas and a bathrobe over his arm, and a pair of slippers in his hand. "Take these. Maria will see to your things."

"Very well. Thank you." And Bäni looked his friend in the eyes, which seemed small under the bushy brows, unfathomable, strangely colorless above the fine network of purple veins that covered his cheeks. Bäni now placed all of his confidence in the exceptional calm radiated by the broad peasant face, not to mention the spark of cunning that shone through now and then.

"I'm in the library. Come down when you're finished. You can tell me what happened," said Rusterholz with an amused smile. He saw no reason to take any of this too seriously. Even in the episode at the airport, Caesar's pride had been hurt more than anything else.

Bäni leaned back in the bathtub and watched the huge man depart. He looked like a bear. He had always found it paradoxical that Wotan had ended up in plastic surgery, and had become a professor. Solely from his appearance, Bäni would have taken him for a forest ranger or a veterinarian. And if he envied the man anything, it was the considerable inheritance that Rusterholz had come into at the sale of his father's estate; but today Bäni envied the ease with which Wotan had mastered his life, and above all his ability to solve problems.

"Whisky?" Rusterholz asked, as Bäni entered the room in a dark blue bathrobe.

"Yes, I could use one."

FELIX METTLER

Bäni stood somewhat lost among the massive oak furniture of the large room. To the left was an entire wall of bookshelves, also of oak. The bar where Rusterholz had just poured the whisky was at the back of the room. And to the right a number of pictures were hung around an open hearth, crowding right up to the ceiling. Rusterholz placed the two glasses in front of the fireplace on a small table, inlaid with a marble chessboard. This was where he spent his evenings at home. Here he solved chess problems, read chess books, replayed master matches, often until well after midnight. And so now too the two professors sat down at the table, as they did on the last Friday of every month, to play a game before the evening meal. Bäni always lost, but it gave Wotan joy, it was like a gift to his host. It was always only a matter of how long he could hold Rusterholz off.

Bäni began his prolonged story, admitting that he had forgotten about the Château Latour, nor did he deny his fear of what Götze's death might mean. That was the reason, after all, for his excursion to the Sihl. An irrational act on the spur of the moment, as he now called it. Rusterholz listened carefully and was silent except for brief exclamations of surprise that eventually were replaced by stronger words. He realized that this time it was a more serious matter than Caesar's reputation or credibility. This time it concerned nothing less than murder. He quickly considered a few other possibilities that he kept to himself, among them that Götze could have been placed in the trunk beforehand, but he found this unbelievable and, more important, illogical. Who would be so crazy as to park Götze's car in front of Caesar's door afterward, with the intention of drawing suspicion to him? Caesar would scarcely have allowed the car to remain there, he thought.

80

"What do you think was the cause of Götze's death?" Rusterholz asked, after Bäni had finished his report and fallen silent for a while.

"I have no idea! A heart attack, perhaps."

"That's wishful thinking," Rusterholz noted, without even a smile. The situation was too serious.

"Would you take back the wine?" Bäni asked suddenly. "It mustn't get out that the bottle was mine."

So, the bottle. That was on Caesar's mind as well. "My fingerprints must be on the pieces of broken glass, I'm the one who removed the bottles from the rack, after all," Rusterholz said, reflecting. "That's not a problem. I simply gave Götze a bottle."

"What!" Bäni sat bolt upright in his chair. "Did you do that?"

"No, of course not. Calm down. Only in case the police should identify my fingerprints."

"I see."

"But what if *your* fingerprints are on it?"

"Wouldn't they have been smeared by the wine?"

"It's possible. And if not?"

"Then it was I who gave Götze the bottle."

"That won't do," Rusterholz said after brief consideration. "You would have told the commissioner that when the two of you discussed the wine. You would have had to, if you were innocent. Good God," he said. "If they find anything, Caesar, you're in deep!"

"I need an alibi for tonight," Bäni said, changing the topic. "Would you provide me with one?"

Rusterholz found this request an obligation, coming as it did from a friend and a colleague who desperately needed help. It wasn't quite right of Caesar, of course— he should have waited for him to offer. But Rusterholz was in a quandary. On the one hand, Caesar was a friend he could not desert. On the other hand, he would incriminate himself if he willingly intervened to conceal a crime. The old dilemma between friendship and the law. "You've got to get an examination, Caesar! It's probably a circulatory problem in your cerebral cortex. It can be controlled with medication."

Bäni nodded several times and looked at his friend expectantly.

"This cannot be allowed to happen again, not under any circumstances," Rusterholz said adamantly. "Otherwise everything will be in vain."

"Yes, Wotan, you're right of course. I know a good neurologist."

Rusterholz stared at the table, at the sixty-four black-and-white squares, and ordered the pieces in his mind. Caesar had gotten himself into a difficult situation. His king was in danger. It was clear that Caesar would want to place a rook in front of it. The queens were out of the game. His opponent's bishops and knights were well positioned, threatening to gain the upper hand. It didn't look good, especially since no major mistakes could be expected from the other side. He had to try for a draw, perhaps force a stalemate. And the price? In a defeat everything was lost. That was clear. But what was to be gained if caution was the prime necessity? Where was the recognition, the praise for a masterful move? No, he didn't like this kind of game. He would have to fight it out. But that would mean taking Caesar down. "Someone could have seen you on the Sihl, when you fell asleep on the bench."

"That's unlikely."

"So! How long have you been here with me, then?"

"Since ... since around eight-thirty. Wotan, I'll never forget this."

"It's all right," Rusterholz waved him off. "I don't know anything. I've simply done you a favor without asking questions. Do you understand? I assumed something about a woman, if anyone asks. But I don't know anything! Is that understood?" Only when Bäni nodded repeatedly and vehemently did Rusterholz stick out his large paw, which his friend shook, visibly moved.

The rain beat against the window as fiercely as before, as if on this one night the sky wanted to make up for everything it had neglected for weeks. Rusterholz proceeded to calculate coldly which points in this affair spoke for Caesar and which spoke against him. In addition to the location of Götze's car, there was the lack of motive, a major point, he declared. Bäni admitted that he had disliked Götze for various reasons, above all for his eager subservience. On the other hand, he couldn't deny having made good use of the man's boundless ambition. Rusterholz listened to this with a certain satisfaction, saw it as a trump that he advised Caesar to use when the time was right. His colleagues needed to notice what a loss he had suffered at Götze's death. But any charge brought against him now was largely a matter of fate, Rusterholz considered further, and of what the police would find. At the moment they themselves could only take precautionary measures, but in the future they would have to play defensively, anticipate the commissioner's moves. "Let's assume the fingerprints on the glass can't be identified. That's a risk we have to take!"

Bäni nodded.

"The rain will wash away anything at the Sihl, the body excluded—there will be nothing left they can use."

"My car is totally filthy. It has to be washed, and cleaned inside."

"Let me take care of that!"

It was already after midnight when Maria appeared. She stood in the door, pale, dressed in black, and announced in her deep vibrato that the clothes had been cleaned and the guest room was prepared.

"Professor Cesare arrived at eight-thirty, and we'll forget about the clothes." Rusterholz said this quietly as if it were totally unimportant.

"Capito! Buona notte."

"Buona notte e grazie mille." Bäni regretted that he had no money on him at the moment. "I'll leave her two hundred francs," he said, after Maria had gone.

"You don't need to give her any money. I pay her, and I pay her well." When it came to his cook Rusterholz saw himself as a patron, a benefactor of superior Italian artistic creations.

"But for her silence. She's supporting my alibi, after all."

"You can't buy Maria! She's an artist through and through, she'll either do it or she won't, basta. Bring her a gift the next time you come. Without explaining why. That will make her happy."

9

It was a morning like the preceding ones, sunny, but slightly cooler. The only signs of the storm of the night before were the leaves and buds scattered on the ground and the rocky soil that had flooded up from the gardens. Sonder took the steps to work easily; he reached the crest where the marvelous fir stood without having to pause for breath. The tree had lost a branch the width of a muscular thigh. It lay on the lawn among a number of large pinecones. Looking closer, Sonder saw that the point of breakage showed some rot, but only a bit, there was no reason to fear for the tree. Relieved, he continued on his way, not worrying about what awaited him, but rather curious.

The professor appeared at coffee break, which he seldom did, and the talk that for three days now had centered on one topic stopped suddenly. He didn't wish to disturb them, Bäni said, but here he had them all assembled in one place. And he wasn't disturbing anyone, of course. They were all eager for first-hand information.

"Doctor Götze's car was found last night, amazingly, on the street where I live," Bäni began. Embarrassed faces all around. "It's a mystery to me, as well. I have no idea what Doctor Götze was doing there." The professor's

FELIX METTLER

agitation, given the extraordinary situation, was a surprise to no one. "In all likelihood the car was parked there during our party. I must have overlooked it. The police are baffled too. I've learned from the commissioner that they're going to search the area around my house for clues. Which will not be easy after a rainstorm. At any rate, my house was not broken into, but the police are checking to see if anyone attempted it. That's all I know at the moment. But I'll keep you informed, to avoid unnecessary rumors."

Bäni immediately returned to his office; he was expecting a call at any moment. He was sure that it would not be long before Götze was found. He felt that he had sounded convincing to his staff, and that his suggestion that someone might have wanted to break in had worked. Without having said anything specific, Bäni now believed himself the source of rumors that would put him in a good light. Each time the phone rang he jumped, quickly collecting himself before he lifted the receiver. He wanted to appear affected by the news, but not overly anxious. But to his surprise no call came.

Sonder too was surprised that there had been no word of the body. Was it still in the trunk, as yet undiscovered, or had its discovery been kept quiet? To protect Bäni, perhaps? Or to be able to conduct the investigation in peace? He felt no pangs of conscience. Furthermore, he was convinced that he had done what was necessary for his own existence—self-defense, that is, which was his right. The fact that he had felt better ever since, that he was free of pain, supported this view.

The commissioner arrived at the clinic late that afternoon. He informed Bäni that nothing had been found in the area around his house, nor at the house itself. Nor had the lab been able to learn anything from the search of the car, as far as he knew. The fingerprints they found matched those on the books and maps in Götze's brief-case. No other prints had been found, he added, but that was not necessarily significant. The fact that whoever had been driving had worn gloves—which the lab had told him—Häberli kept to himself.

That evening Bäni called his friend to report on what had happened thus far, and on what he had found out from the commissioner. Rusterholz listened in silence, then said it appeared that they had cleared a hurdle in respect to the wine bottle. He assured him that the rest of the bottles were back on the wine rack where they had spent the last twenty years. Bäni had picked them up at home that morning and delivered them to him at an agreed-upon meeting place.

"So we'll assume that Götze's body was carried away by the high water," Rusterholz later said. "I can't imagine otherwise."

"That wouldn't be so bad."

Rusterholz warned him against being too optimistic. "Let's wait and see what happens with the body, it will have to turn up sometime. I've yet to catch any piranhas in the Sihl." He said this grimly, irritated that it was the Sihl Caesar had chosen to throw the body into. Lake Zurich would have done just as well.

Friday too passed with no new discoveries. At coffee break, Sonder again listened to people's various theories. They seemed to be equally divided between homicide and suicide; only Zimmerli still believed that the assistant director had run off. When asked his opinion, Sonder shrugged his shoulders and said he couldn't really imag-ine any of it. The fact that he and his own problem received scarcely any attention in the light of this new business was fine with him. Only Pat Wyss and Doctor Thalmann asked occasionally how he felt.

Bäni had spent another day in the vain hope of hearing that Götze had been found. He should have been happy, another day without the body having been located could only work to his advantage. But there was something else, an insecurity he felt increasingly—the doubt that events had really occurred as he thought they had, and as he had told Wotan they had. Some of it seemed strange to him, improbable even, when he thought of the scene at the Hirschfels. He would have liked some proof of his own credibility—for himself, but especially for Wotan. For even though he believed his friend would stick with him through thick and thin, he was still afraid that Wotan would betray his trust and abandon him if Götze were not found soon.

Finally, on Saturday morning, something happened. The commissioner called Bäni at home: a fisherman had found a body at the Sihl, and the description fit Götze. The location Häberli mentioned was, by Bäni's calculation, one or two kilometers from the Hirschfels.

"Well, for God's sake, how did he get there?" Bäni sounded upset. So Wotan was right! The high water must have dislodged the body and carried it a little way downriver.

"That's just what we'd like to know. I simply wanted to inform you that your colleague is dead. It can scarcely come as a surprise."

"How do you mean that?" Bäni asked, startled. Did the commissioner think he knew something?

"Well, there was the suspicion from the beginning that a crime had been committed, isn't that so?"

"Yes, that's so. But are you sure it was a crime?" Bäni felt compelled to say something—something harmless, of course.

"I'm hoping that forensics will be able to tell us more," Häberli answered.

"So do I!"

Then Bäni thanked the commissioner for his prompt report and asked to be kept informed of developments. Häberli agreed to do so.

Rusterholz, immediately apprised of the latest news, advised caution. He found Bäni's idea of calling the head of forensics too risky, even if he knew him well, and advised against it. In the end, he said, Bäni could no longer differentiate between what he should know and what he shouldn't, and that was dangerous. The thing was complicated enough already.

10

It was late Saturday afternoon—Gottfried Sonder had slept for a good two hours. Napped. He wanted to be fresh for that evening. He snipped a few branches from his rosebushes in the garden, taking anything that was blooming or had buds that were opening. What did it matter, he thought, looking at the stripped bushes, he had to start clearing out things in the next few days anyway. Everything had to go. He had given notice on his apartment. His lease expired at the end of July. Sonder put the roses on the table near the bag with his bathing suit. Pat had suggested that he bring his suit with him, had insisted upon it when he hesitated. He was glad to be spending the evening with the two young doctors. Pat Wyss and Doctor Thalmann had played an essential part in his recuperation. Had it not been for his conversations with them at the beginning of the week, things would not have happened as they did. Thalmann had spurred him on to battle, and Pat had helped him identify the enemy. And surely no one other than they would ever be able to establish the motive for his deed. He could not count on their approval, but he could not imagine that they would present a danger to him, not these two, of all people, who had always treated him with respect, even with favor.

Thalmann came by around five to pick him up. They drove through the city past Bellevue, then along the lake road to Herrliberg. Together they looked for the yellow house with the red beech in front.

When Bruno Thalmann rang the bell they heard barking, and moments later a dangerous-looking dog— it was a German boxer—started running back and forth behind the fence. It calmed down only when Pat came out.

"Come in," Pat said, after opening the gate. "Hercule won't hurt you." She was delighted at the bouquet of roses. She would take them with her to the office on Monday, she said.

As the three of them strolled across the lawn the dog followed, a tennis ball in its mouth, and when they stopped at the edge of the lake he laid the ball at Sonder's feet. Bowing his head, he looked back and forth from Sonder to the ball, expectant, his body ready to leap. Sonder gave the ball a kick and the dog shot out after it.

"Hercule has an infallible sense of people," Pat said to Sonder, "he chooses only the nice ones to play with."

Sonder smiled in embarrassment. He didn't know whether to thank Pat or the dog for this compliment.

They sat down on a wall and discussed the beauty of their surroundings, the weather, the lake, the sailboats with their slack sails, until Pat suggested going for a swim. She preceded her guests into the house to show them where they could change. Sonder hung back.

"I'm all right. I'm not much of a swimmer," he said, as Pat invited him in.

"But you brought your suit," Pat said, pointing to the bag he had with him.

"Yes, but . . ."

Pat went up to him and put her hand on his arm. "We're alone here, Herr Sonder, and doctors know what scars look like."

What could he say to that? She wouldn't take no for an answer. Sonder picked up his bag. She was right, of course, he told himself; there was no cause for inhibitions. But somehow he didn't view Pat primarily as a doctor—she was also an attractive young woman. Particularly now, without her white coat.

When they swam out with Sonder, Thalmann asked several times if everything was all right, and whether he was overtaxing himself. Sonder, who had been a good swimmer in his youth, waved this off. He was enjoying the cool water.

Pat made drinks. They chatted for a while, and it occurred to Sonder that no one had mentioned Götze, though his disappearance had been the chief topic of conversation for days. He asked himself if this was deliberate, whether they had decided beforehand not to broach the subject today. Nor was Sonder's scar mentioned, large and conspicuous as it was on his hairy body. Pat and Thalmann didn't seem to notice.

Around seven they decided to begin preparations for dinner. After they changed, Bruno Thalmann helped out in the kitchen while Sonder got the charcoal fire started. Then he threw the ball across the grass for the dog, who was inexhaustible.

Sonder looked up at the sound of a loud, rhythmic clapping coming from the lake. It was two swans. With a flapping of wings, their necks outstretched and their black feet trailing behind them, the swans finally rose over the water. Their heavy bodies lifted into the air with long, majestic movements. Sonder saw the awkward transition from dignified swimming to powerful flight as antediluvian, the transition from one perfect image to another. He watched the birds for a long time.

When Pat and Thalmann came out of the house— she with a tray of dishes and he with a platter of sausages and lamb chops—Sonder felt that something had happened. Their faces and gestures indicated it.

"They found him," Pat said excitedly, even before she had placed the tray on the table. "It was on the radio. They found him in the Sihl."

"Where?" Sonder exclaimed. He couldn't have heard right. At the same moment he reminded himself to be careful. One impulsive reaction could betray him.

"In the Sihl," Pat repeated. "They don't know the cause of death."

"The police are looking for witnesses who might have seen him Tuesday evening . . ." Thalmann said.

". . . or who might have observed something suspicious at the Sihl," Pat finished.

Why the Sihl? Sonder asked himself in amazement. How did he get there? Could it be a stratagem to cover Bäni? But surely not at the cost of having to look for witnesses who might have seen something at the Sihl. Or had Bäni taken the body there himself, in order to avoid complications? But why would he do something like that, what did he have to be afraid of? Sonder had known that he was putting Bäni in a predicament, and he had been curious as to how the professor would get himself out of it. But he had never reckoned with Bäni trying to get rid of the body. At any rate, this turn of events wasn't inopportune. As he stood at the grill trying to make sense of the news, he listened with one ear to the conversation of the others.

". . . someone like him would lose it if he thought he

wasn't going to get the position. With his warped ambition . . ." Pat obviously thought it was a suicide, the
motive of which was professional. "That's why his car
was parked outside Caesar's house," she argued.

"But after all, what do we know about his private life,
his past? He said something once. I don't know . . ."
Thalmann seemed to be leaning more toward a problem
with a relationship. At any rate, he rejected the idea of
suicide. Götze just wasn't the type, he said.

Sonder busied himself with the coals. What he caught
of the conversation was reassuring. He immediately dismissed the thought that they were trying to trick him—
Pat would have given it away. He was sure that her eyes
could never conceal suspicion.

Before they began eating, Pat suggested that they not
discuss the matter further. She wanted to enjoy the evening, the food, and their time together—they would find
out more on Monday in any case. The two men agreed.
After the meal Pat suggested that her two guests take the
rowboat out. They would find it in the wooden house
under the willows, she said; in the meantime she would
clean up a bit. But the two men offered to help and carried
the dishes into the kitchen, where Sonder immediately
began to wash them. He had forgotten that there were
machines to do that.

Pat was the first to take the oars. She rowed through
the water effortlessly, told them of the battles she used
to have on the lake with the neighbors' children, and
seemed not at all tired by the rowing. After a while, when
they were already some distance from the shore, Sonder
asked to relieve her and then insisted upon it, ignoring
Thalmann's comments about his health. Sonder began
rowing carefully at first, and then more forcefully, having
to fight against going in circles as the other two laughed.

"Don't overdo it, Herr Sonder," Thalmann said with concern after a few minutes. "You should save your strength."

"Not at all! I need to get in shape again," Sonder answered, his voice strained. "I'm going to need it."

Was this really the man he had spoken to at the beginning of the week? Thalmann asked himself. In the few days since then he must have gone through a complete transformation, he suddenly seemed so full of life and confident. Pat too was amazed. During their last conversation he had been evasive, hadn't wanted to talk about the future, and now he was bringing it up himself. She was happy for him without reflecting further on the change. Thalmann rowed the boat back, somewhat awkwardly, but with Pat's help he steered it into the boathouse.

"You row well, Herr Sonder. Do you feel tired?" Pat asked as they were sitting in the garden enjoying the warm evening. Pat and Sonder were drinking beer, and Thalmann mineral water, as he had to drive.

"No, not at all," Sonder said matter-of-factly, as if he had never been ill.

"You said you have to get in shape. So you must have something specific in mind?" Pat asked cautiously.

Sonder nodded. And after hesitating for a moment he said drily, "I want to stand on top of Kilimanjaro one more time." He had decided to go straight to the heart of the matter.

"What!" Thalmann blurted out in horror. "It's over 16,000 feet high."

"Why not?" Pat gave her colleague a disapproving look.

"Nineteen thousand one hundred sixty feet," Sonder smiled in amusement. "I was there eleven years ago."

Thalmann remembered their conversation from Monday. Sonder had mentioned mountain climbing. He wanted to climb until he could go no further was what he had said. Neither forward nor back. "So you want to conquer it again?" he asked, hoping that Sonder would contradict him.

"No, not conquer. No, I'm no longer strong enough for that." A mysterious smile played at his mouth. "In old age you no longer fight the mountain, you let the mountain lift you up."

"I don't understand what you mean." Thalmann was perturbed.

"I wouldn't have thought it possible either, earlier. But then I experienced it, and it was on Kilimanjaro. From the moment I spied it from the Masai steppes, I felt it. Something special." Sonder looked past Thalmann as he spoke, his face transfigured. He had recognized Kilimanjaro at first glance from far away. Unknown and yet familiar, as a face can sometimes seem in a strange land. The mountain appeared to be a friend, then a father, and in the end he had seen it as the great spirit that was everywhere, in one form or another. But the spirit had never appeared to him so clearly before. Sonder spoke devoutly, pausing occasionally to collect himself. The mountain had attracted him, it pulled him up the broad plain like a magnet. First through the lush rain forest, damp and rotting, smelling of death and of conception, creatures creeping and crawling on its floor, butterflies in the air, apes screaming in the trees. The images crowded in on Sonder more intensely than ever before. The constant change in the vegetation from one level to the next, becoming more and more sparse, the plants more and more exotic. And he remembered the red gladioli radiating from a narrow ravine—like a symbol. Soon there was only grass and lichen-covered rocks. He accepted everything the mountain offered him, soaked it up, every movement, every sign. Higher up was the black sand desert strewn with fantastic bluffs, a moon landscape veiled in tattered fog. He had felt neither fatigue nor the cold nor the pain that were otherwise common at these heights. And then came the climb by night in the newly fallen snow, each step taken within the circle of the flashlight, following the rhythm of the mountain hour after hour. When he came to the edge of the crater there was a dawn as it must have been millions of years before, as on the first day of creation. He felt a childlike wonder; he was incapable of speech. Farther along the crater lay the bluish pipe organs of primeval ice, the incredible music of absolute silence. And then the peak, close to heaven, thousands of feet above the plains that teemed with game. Overwhelmed by the feeling of being at one with the mountain, he stood there, proud and humble to be a small part of something so great.

It was quiet for a while after Sonder stopped talking and stared at the lake, lost in thought. It was twilight, lights were turned on here and there.

Pat was touched by the way Sonder had told his tale, and also impressed by his accomplishment. She spontaneously thought of the old men of Asia, who were able to span bows requiring a strength that was said to surpass the power of the human body alone. Had Sonder attained something like that as well? Was he capable of taking the thousands of small steps that would add up to one great step? The man never ceased to amaze her. "What an experience," she said, adding almost reproachfully, "And you never told us about it."

"Who would understand it?"

"I would," Pat said.

"We would," Thalmann corrected her.

"Then you can also understand that I must return."

"Yes, of course."

"How long will you stay?" Thalmann asked guile-lessly.

"I won't return." Sonder said this without emotion, knowing that it would cause surprise, if not dismay.

"And the checkups . . ." Thalmann said immediately.

He had anticipated this objection. "No more check-ups. They're no longer necessary."

"But of course they're necessary. You know that . . ."

"You talked me into the operation, Herr Thalmann, and I am grateful for that." Sonder remained unmoved.

Pat looked from one to the other, undecided as to how she should enter the conversation. As a doctor she had to support Bruno, had to encourage Sonder to main-tain his health. But on the other hand, what right did they have to dictate to an old man—particularly this old man—what he had to do?

"I don't understand that you . . . now, when every-thing . . ." What's the point, Thalmann asked himself, Sonder knows quite well what the situation is. And now is not the time anyway.

"It is my wish to spend the time left to me in a place where life is . . . spirited, and where death has meaning." Sonder in no way sounded despondent or resigned, as one might have expected hearing him talk about death. On the contrary, he seemed relieved. He continued to stroke the dog, who had laid his head in his lap.

When Thalmann, worried, fell quiet, Pat looked at Sonder, her mouth open, still unsure of what to make of his statement. Had he merely spoken without thinking, or was there more to it—knowledge, even wisdom? She had to assume so. Also, that his moving story of Africa and his desire to live and die there were intertwined. "It's that they value nature there, isn't it? Life in nature," she said, in an attempt to continue the conversation.

"Primal nature, where nothing is yet finished. Everything is in motion. Nature is still seeking out new forms. Yes. Here, nothing new can develop, in our overfertilized fields and leveled forests. Here everything has turned to stone, the earth and the sky, and our thinking as well. It's no longer a place I want to live, much less die. The hospital made that clear to me." They could hear laughter coming from the house next door. "Death in a white hospital room would be senseless to me, the crucifix on the wall notwithstanding. It too has turned to stone. But there," Sonder pointed his arm into the distance, "from death comes new life, visible, palpable. There things still decay. And things have to decay so that new life can emerge."

"And stones don't decay," Pat said softly.

"No, stones don't decay," Sonder repeated louder.

Thalmann stood up and took a few steps toward the lake. It had gotten dark, there was no moon. A band of light defined the opposite shore. A bat flew back and forth in front of his face. Thalmann thought about Sonder, about his altered behavior, the abstruse ideas he had had since the onset of his illness. Sonder had always had original ideas, he couldn't deny that, but up to now his thinking had been contained in a logical framework. What he now planned, however, was crazy. He would be the one to suffer from it in the end, Thalmann was sure of that. He would have to speak to him again, soberly, when they were alone. Not now, nor after their drive back. They would not come to an agreement today. He also had to speak with Pat. With her help he could bring Sonder to his senses. Yes, his senses. Thalmann didn't understand what he now heard Sonder saying: that to answer the cry of the owl from deep within, from the lungs or the stomach—becoming for an instant an owl oneself—one could see what a bird sees.

At Pat's request Sonder repeated the owl's call several times more. She was delighted. And when the neighbors fell silent because everyone—she assumed—was listening for the cry of the owl, Pat broke out in a hearty laugh.

When Pat refilled their glasses again, Thalmann remarked that they would have to think about leaving soon. But he met with strenuous protest. She was having a great time, Pat said, she didn't want them to go. But if Thalmann had to, she would take care of Sonder. The last train to Zurich left at 11:30. And besides, he could stay the night if he wished. Sonder agreed to her suggestion. He felt better than he had in a long time.

After she had shown Bruno Thalmann out, Pat sat down again with Sonder, curious to hear more of Africa. She had spent a month with an uncle in Mombasa after graduating from high school, and had gone on safari from there twice. But Sonder seemed to be talking about something else when he spoke of the sun glittering on the parched steppes, of the magnificent cloud banks, the heavy rainstorms and lush, flowering vegetation, of seasons compressed into days. She had seen elephants and giraffes, lions and zebras and warthogs—as in a zoo, it now occurred to her. But she hadn't experienced Africa, the Africa Sonder was talking about.

He recounted the hunt for cheetahs, relived it, described the perfect harmony in their blend of power and elegance, took long minutes to describe what had happened in seconds. The hunters approaching their prey. An impala fleeing in mortal fear. The chase. Then the leap. The fall. Sonder experienced it all again, this hunt;

she could feel what the hunt had meant to him, how for him it culminated in the union of two bodies. All the laws of life were contained in this one brief moment, he said in closing. He seemed lost in thought. Exhausted, but happy. "Life emerges from what is dead, what appears dead. That's how it is in the tropics. It should be like that everywhere." And as he thought of the rules of nature, he thought of Götze. Hadn't Götze attempted to create new life from someone else's death? Where did the difference lie? But if it had been natural for Götze to do so, he told himself, then his own act was easy to justify as well. It remained what it was: a defense. The body is permitted to fight off parasites; the prey can attack the hunter. Had he ever borne a grudge against the wild boar he had shot—the one that had smashed his knee—for the injury he had caused him? No, he had only respected it.

"Are human beings actually responsible for their environment, or is it the other way around, does the environment make the human?" Pat didn't expect an answer. "What would Zurich look like in the tropics, what would a tropicalized Bahnhofstrasse look like?" She had quickly latched on to the word. I'd like to tropicalize everything, someone had said.

Sonder laughed. He thought of Medan or Guayaquil, or a combination of the two cities. Cities in the tropics had something in common. "Zurich would survive," Sonder said, "it would survive according to the laws of the jungle." He envisioned a tangle of cars, stray dogs milling through the garbage, vultures at the marble temple of Max Bill, beggars in front of the banks, iguanas at the globe in the park, the train station underpass flooding when it rained, plaster on the sidewalks that had fallen from the facades of the buildings. Buildings, that was to say, that were slowly decaying. "Yes, stones can decay. In the tropics they can decay." He thought of Venice; it should not be saved, the strenuous efforts to do so were a mistake, because then it would be robbed of its charm. At least for him.

Pat was amused. It was fun to make connections between things spontaneously, she loved to imagine the impossible. She never would have thought it would be Sonder, this man who appeared so ordinary, who, of all people, would be entertaining her with such fantasies. It was she who had invited him to distract him, to get him out of his doldrums. And now this.

"Shall we go into the water again?" Pat asked bluntly.

"Why not?" His stories had made Sonder adventurous.

Pat brought two robes out of the house and soon they were swimming side by side silently, at the same speed. Sonder felt free, totally free. It was as if he had removed more than his clothing. Back on the bank he struggled to keep his balance on the slippery stones. Twice he had to support himself with his hands until Pat grabbed his arm. Sonder gladly allowed this, and they left the water together. And as they slowly crossed the yard toward the house her hand lay on his shoulder, no longer as support, and she left it there, as she would have touched the coat of a friendly animal.

"Thank you," Sonder said, as Pat handed him the robe, and then was shocked that he had addressed her in the familiar. "Oh, excuse me, I . . ."

"You don't have to apologize, Göpf. It's fine," Pat laughed. "You have my permission."

It was long past midnight. Sitting on the edge of his bed, Sonder looked for a moment around the room— Pat's brother's, who, she had told him, was spending a year in America. Then he lay down and thought about the evening. He had talked a lot, he felt, much more than usual. Yes, he had enjoyed their company.

The next morning when Pat opened the curtains, she saw Sonder sitting in the rowboat not far from shore. She called to him and waved, and he waved back. After breakfast she took him to the train station. There they read a report in the Sunday paper carrying the headline "Missing Physician Found Dead in the Sihl." The article said that Götze was already dead when he was put into the water, and that foul play was suspected, even though the cause of death had not yet been determined. Sonder, forgetting himself, shook his head several times. There was a picture of Götze accompanying the article—a flattering one, Pat noted—and it was stated that witnesses were being sought who had seen Götze after 6:00 P.M. on Tuesday, or who had noticed anything unusual at the Sihl River. Sonder shrugged his shoulders involuntarily.

11

At eight on Monday morning Häberli and Manz were sitting across from one another in the commissioner's office. Each had a copy of the preliminary autopsy report in his hand, and they were going over it point by point. Manz was underlining what he considered important while the commissioner was scribbling on a sheet of paper. There were several names on the sheet, and a line that represented the route from Bäni's house to the Sihl. Drawing was part of Häberli's method of solving complicated cases. And he felt that finding an explanation for Götze's death was not going to be simple.

The coroner's report stated that roughly one day had gone by after Götze had died before his body was placed in the water, and that it had been in the water for three days. So the time of death coincided with Götze's disappearance, Manz calculated. From the scratches on the body it could be deduced that it had been dragged along the river for a considerable stretch. A fracture of the right zygomatic arch had probably originated at the time of death, but there was no sign of further injuries. That meant that the death had not been a violent one, a fact that Häberli always found particularly challenging to an investigation. Neither of the men regarded the appendix scar or the rough skin on the victim's back and buttocks as significant. The report closed with the usual statement that a determination of the cause of death could not be made until histological and toxicological examinations had been performed. Häberli did not mention that he did not expect much from the examinations in this case. It was a feeling he would not have been able to explain.

"Where do you think the key to this murder lies?" the commissioner asked.

"In the clinic," Manz answered without hesitation. "The lack of an apparent cause of death points to an expert and to premeditation, and the dead man's car parked in front of the professor's house points to someone who knew the scene."

Häberli's faint nod signified that he was in agreement with this line of thought. "I've informed the clinic we're coming at nine."

He and Manz had been to Götze's apartment again on Saturday afternoon, but had found nothing useful except the address of his former wife. Nor could they learn anything from the super or the neighbors, all of whom claimed not to have known Götze well. Manz then called Götze's ex-wife. She was listed under the name Bernasconi, spoke German with a Slavic accent, and did not seem particularly affected by her first husband's death. They had not been in contact with each other for two years, she said, and she could not tell them anything about his life or the company he had kept lately. Asked about their child, she answered candidly that after the divorce her husband, more out of meanness than anything else, had challenged his paternity, which, on examination, had been established nevertheless. After this,

the hope of learning anything about Götze's habits and
friends rested on what they could learn from his colleagues at the clinic.

Professor Bäni had given orders that the library be
used for the upcoming interrogations. Sonder was carrying a third armchair into the room when the two
plainclothesmen entered, accompanied by Bäni. Bäni
instructed Sonder to wait outside and show in those people the detectives wished to speak to. Sonder walked
slowly up and down the corridor, his hands clasped behind his back. So these were the bloodhounds who would
try to track him down, he thought. But not only him—
for after all, he had nothing to do with what had happened on the Sihl. They seemed nice, he decided; both
had given him a friendly nod.

"I hope you understand that it's necessary for us to
nose around a bit," Häberli began after they had sat
down, the professor on one side of the table, the police
on the other.

"But of course," Bäni said, eager to help, and he
pushed across to the commissioner a piece of paper on
which the names of all the staff were listed. He was at
the top of the list, then Doctor Thalmann and Pat Wyss,
then the secretaries, the lab personnel, and last, the autopsy workers Zimmerli and Sonder.

"We know next to nothing about Doctor Götze," Häberli continued. "We'd like to form some kind of picture
of him first, learn something of his habits and character."

"Doctor Götze! He was obsessed with his work, a
workaholic as the Americans say." Bäni portrayed him
as an extremely reliable colleague who would do any
amount of work to further his career. And this had already paid off—he was just at the point of being appointed associate professor at the university. He had

perhaps not been the most talented, Bäni added; he didn't have the imagination it took to become an outstanding diagnostician. But he compensated for that with an amazing store of knowledge. He was a walking encyclopedia, the professor said, lamenting the great loss he himself had suffered at the death of his assistant. Questioned about Götze's relationship with his colleagues, Bäni shrugged his shoulders; his expression said it all. It was not easy for subordinates to work with such a man, he explained; Götze was very demanding. He knew very little about Götze's private life, but didn't think he had much time for one. He wasn't aware of any special predilections, nor of any colleagues he might be seeing outside the clinic.

But the casual tone of the interrogation came to an end when Häberli again asked for exact details concerning the two critical days in question. Bäni spoke more slowly now. Every sentence was well thought out, almost ready for print, with the exception of a few additional comments. He described Tuesday evening as it had transpired, namely, that he had fallen asleep for thirty minutes to an hour and had then driven to the cabin where the party took place. He didn't know the precise time of his return, but it must have been shortly after midnight. He had spent the whole day Wednesday at the Institute and that evening—after their visit—he had driven out to Kilchberg to see his friend Eugene Rusterholz. He had spent the night there, which was not unusual as they liked to have a few drinks together.

Bäni didn't miss the fact that Manz did not react to this information, whereas the commissioner smiled understandingly. Though Häberli had asked all the questions up to that point, Bäni had directed his answers to Manz for the most part, as if it were Manz above all whom he wanted to convince of the truth of his statement.

"You've seen the wine bottle already! Do you perhaps recognize this pipe?" Häberli asked, as he took the shards of glass and the metal tube from a plastic bag and placed them on the table.

Bäni quickly responded in the negative. He thought about inquiring about the significance of the object, but then decided against it.

"That's all I have," Häberli said, and turned to Manz. "Do you have anything further?"

Manz nodded. "You've surely given some thought as to why Doctor Götze's car was parked in front of your house?"

"Yes, of course," Bäni responded sharply, showing that he felt the question to be impertinent.

"And you have no idea how it could have come to this odd . . . let us say, coincidence?" Manz fixed his eyes on the scar on the professor's face. Scalpels left behind prettier scars and fewer gold teeth, he thought to himself, and doctors handled them better than a fencing foil.

"No," Bäni answered after a brief pause, "unless someone wants to incriminate me."

"Did Doctor Götze visit your home now and then?"

"Two or three times, by invitation only. Otherwise no, never." His first impression had been correct. The man was unpleasant, even dangerous.

Manz motioned to Häberli that he had no further questions. The commissioner thanked the professor and handed him Götze's lecture notes from his file, the ones that Bäni had been looking for. Now all Bäni had to do was read the chapter on vascular disease.

The commissioner ignored Bäni's offer to have Doctor Thalmann sent in. Instead he asked him to send in the man whom Bäni had instructed to help them. From the

way Sonder entered the room, approached them, introduced himself, and sat down, Häberli thought him reserved rather than reticent, and certainly not subservient.
He found Sonder's name at the bottom of the list, which
obviously had been made out in order of status in the
department.

"So you were at the party on Tuesday! What did you
. . ." The commissioner paused when he saw Sonder
shaking his head.

"No, I wasn't there!" Sonder said decisively.

"Oh! And why not?"

"I was watching the soccer game."

"On television?"

"No. At the stadium."

"So you don't think much of these departmental parties." Häberli smiled. "Why not?"

"Doctor Götze." Sonder swallowed. "I naturally assumed that he would be there."

Manz, still busy making notes on their talk with the
professor, raised his head. Sonder avoided the commissioner's question of whether he had had problems with
Götze recently by explaining that he had been back at
work only for a week. Questioned on his absence, he
mentioned the operation, his stay at the sanatorium in
Davos, and also his retirement in one month. When
Manz wanted to know if anyone had seen him at the
soccer game, Sonder gave him the name of Director Zurbuchen, whom he had met in the tram before the game,
as well as that of a neighbor he had spoken with briefly
on his way home.

"And Wednesday? What did you do on Wednesday?"

"I went to work and then I went home, where I remained for the rest of the evening." And to the question
of whether there was anyone who could confirm that, he

answered with a smile, "Not unless you count two cats."

After Sonder stated that he had never seen the objects on the table, his interrogation was over. Afterward he showed his colleagues into the library: Imelda Stäuble, Doctor Thalmann, Oskar Zimmerli, and the women who worked in the lab. No one had anything particularly good to say about Götze, least of all the laboratory workers. Thalmann was very adroit. Nothing he said spoke ill of Götze, but nothing spoke positively either. Imelda Stäuble, powdered and made up like a doll, appeared quite nervous and constantly played with her hair, which was piled up artfully on her head. She answered the commissioner's question of how she got along with Götze with petty details. Häberli saw no reason to press the point, and Manz had no further questions.

In the end, only Pat Wyss was left. She had been informed of the police's visit by the professor and been asked to come in a little earlier that day. When she entered the library Manz repressed a soft cry of surprise. He knew her from sight, quite well, it could be said, though they had scarcely spoken. Pat greeted the commissioner and held out her hand to Manz with a laugh.

"I don't even know your name," she said.

"Adrian. And you are Patrizia." It was on the sheet of paper.

"Pat," she corrected him.

In his official capacity Manz could not use the familiar address that otherwise would have been natural. "We see each other regularly at the health club," he explained to the commissioner.

"Do you also fence?" Häberli asked.

"No, jazz ballet. We see each other Tuesdays at an exercise class or in the sauna," Pat answered breezily.

This last part hadn't been necessary. Manz was visibly

embarrassed. It was a health club sauna, totally proper, but how could he make that clear to Häberli? At any rate, now, in Pat's presence, wasn't the right time. "You weren't there last Tuesday." Manz attempted to make the transition to the particular evening in question. He waited for her statement.

"I consider it a compliment that you noticed."

Manz's expression was strained, his eyes darted about as he searched feverishly for an appropriate answer. Häberli, who could tell that his presence was keeping Manz from replying as he would like to, now stepped in and took over the questioning concerning that evening.

Pat Wyss stated that she had driven to the cabin early, as she was in charge of the preparations. Furthermore, she made no secret of her feelings for Götze, which were even more negative than those of the laboratory workers before her.

"Did Doctor Götze clearly state that he was coming to the party?" Manz asked.

"Yes. He let me know that afternoon that he would be arriving somewhat late."

"Did he say why?"

"He had something to do, he said." She frowned for a moment before correcting herself. "An appointment! Yes, he said he had an appointment."

"An appointment? Can you remember his words exactly?" Manz asked, visibly interested.

"That's how he put it, an appointment, or something similar. Otherwise I wouldn't have thought of a psychiatrist's session when he said it."

An interesting association, Häberli thought to himself, if somewhat lacking in respect. Manz, who liked her openness despite what had just transpired, considered this last statement the most significant. At least they now had a basis for further questions. She didn't know anything about the objects on the table.

"Will I see you tomorrow evening?" Pat asked, as she said good-bye to Adrian Manz.

"Perhaps, if work permits." But it was clear to Manz that only something extraordinary would keep him from his exercise class. When Pat Wyss had closed the door behind her Häberli took out a piece of paper and put a mark by the victim's name.

"Götze doesn't appear to have any friends here," Manz commented.

"He may have been hated. But is that motive enough? I don't think so."

"I'll look into that appointment in any case. It might get us somewhere."

That afternoon Häberli went for a walk at the university. He visited the forensics department first; there was nothing new. Then he dropped by the Institute of Pathology to get the names of those who were in the running for the associate professorship. At the same time, Manz was having a questionnaire sent to all the physicians and dentists in the city asking if any of them were treating a patient by the name of Horst Götze. He grinned when he gave the order to begin with the psychiatrists. He himself would visit the wine merchants. He chose first those stores that specialized in fine French wines. At the second one he found the name Rusterholz on the customer list, Professor Eugene Rusterholz, a name he had already heard once that day.

12

Nothing in the library gave any hint that an interrogation had taken place there the day before. Sonder removed books from the shelves and typed their titles and authors on index cards one letter at a time, using two fingers. Thalmann had suggested this work for him, if he was interested. Why not, Sonder said to himself. The time would pass more quickly if he had something to do. He was climbing the aluminum ladder to replace a few of the books and take down others when the door opened. Bäni's greeting was almost nonexistent, as usual, but that didn't bother Sonder, he had gotten used to it over the years.

"Have you seen the Robbins anywhere?" Bäni walked up and down the shelves nervously.

"Who?" Sonder asked, slightly irritated.

Only then did Bäni seem to notice that it was Sonder standing on the ladder. "A thick book, greenish-blue, rather conspicuous."

"The books from Doctor Götze's office are there." Sonder pointed down at the table. At exactly the spot where yesterday the blowpipe he himself had made had stood, it occurred to him. For a moment he regretted leaving the pipe behind in the car. Not because it could become a piece of evidence in the hands of the police, but rather because he would have liked to add it to his collection. After all, it was part of a weapon that now also belonged to his history. The thought was motivated solely by the collector's impulse toward completeness, since he would not be taking his collection with him when he went away. Sonder had not yet considered what he would do with all his weapons.

"Of course. He hoarded half the library." Bäni found the book he was looking for. As he headed for the door, Robbins in hand, he stopped suddenly under the ladder. "Damned unpleasant situation, eh?"

"Yes!" Sonder asked himself whether Bäni meant his own situation or the one at the Institute.

"You didn't have such an easy time with him either."

"You might say that." If Caesar knew anything he would not be speaking so familiarly. But why was he speaking to him at all? And why did he get rid of the body? Sonder no longer had any doubt that it was Bäni. Was that his method of solving problems? Simply to get rid of whatever was unpleasant? He would have liked to ask. But more important than Caesar's reason for removing the body was the favor the professor had done him, an invaluable favor. It rendered unlikely his own role in Götze's disappearance. How could he have gotten to the Sihl valley?

"Well, he wasn't a pleasant colleague to have," Bäni sighed. "Pathologically ambitious, I would say. Wanted to be a professor and worked like crazy for it. For that only. He would have reached his goal, though he didn't have what it takes." Sonder, also holding a book, half turned to look down at Bäni, who was talking more to himself than to Sonder. "When you work like crazy, you can get a professorship. Anyone can. Unfortunately. But he wouldn't have been satisfied with that for long. He would have wanted to be dean. And then rector. He's free of that compulsion now."

Sonder nodded silently. He asked himself why Caesar was telling him this, him of all people. After the professor had turned suddenly and left the library—again, almost without a word of salutation—Sonder climbed down from the ladder and continued slowly with his work. Why should he wear himself out? It was only makeshift, they had to give him something to do. And the job he had performed for many years before his illness was being done by someone else. He had once imagined that he would be the one to train his successor. But Zimmerli had been employed at this work already, in a hospital in Basel, in pathology; he didn't need any help. Nevertheless, it was nice of Zimmerli to invite him to drop by whenever he wished. But the autopsy room had been his domain for too long. He couldn't imagine standing around there with nothing to do.

It was a quiet day for Sonder in every respect. Nothing new was reported about Götze, and the library had only one additional visitor. Thalmann came in to get a journal. Sonder wasn't embarrassed when Thalmann walked in to find him idly staring out of a window. One deserved a break from busywork. He had actually expected Thalmann to continue his discussion with him; he was almost afraid he would, for Thalmann would never be able to understand him. He had realized that in the interim. For Thalmann, the number of months, weeks, days that remained to a person seemed to count more than the quality of life. And it bothered Sonder that a religious man like Thalmann so much resembled the other doctors in this respect.

"Worried about something?" Sonder asked, when the

doctor had stood beside him for a while, staring out the window in contemplation.

"Caesar has offered me Götze's job."

"Did you take it?"

"Not yet. I asked for some time to think about it. He wants an answer tomorrow."

"Isn't this your big chance?"

"Yes." Thalmann gave a loud sigh. "If Götze had gotten the position at the university it would have been different."

Poor man, Sonder thought, when he was alone again. It was Thalmann who had encouraged him to do battle. Must Thalmann now suffer because it was Götze he had done battle with? He felt truly sorry for him.

13

Hello, Adrian! Anything new?" Pat asked, out of breath from the exercise class that had just ended. She hadn't heard of any new developments that day. What the newspapers had printed she already knew, and Caesar, who she assumed would be the first to hear something, had nothing to report.

"Not much," Manz answered. "But let's find somewhere else where it's more pleasant to talk." Strictly speaking, nothing had been learned since yesterday, at least nothing he could talk about. But why not take advantage of the situation? "Are you going to the sauna?"

"No, I don't need to now." Pat pointed to the dark spots on her jersey. "I've already sweated enough."

"Let's meet later in the Morgensonne."

"All right." Pat looked at her watch. "Say a quarter after seven?"

Standing under the shower, Manz thought neither of Götze nor of Professor Rusterholz, whom he would drop in on the following day. He would not have believed how easily he could be diverted from this delicate task. Even though this was his free time, he was shocked at how unimportant what had been foremost in his mind now seemed.

"You don't really look like a bloodhound," Pat said mischievously as she sat down beside him.

"Nor do you."

"I? How do you mean that?"

"How is a doctor's work any different? To get to the bottom of an illness, you have to invade the private sphere. Where's the difference?"

"But we deal with victims, whereas you deal with perpetrators," she countered indignantly.

"Are you so sure?" Manz answered. "Aren't our perpetrators victims as well—and vice versa, aren't your victims sometimes perpetrators?"

He was right, of course. Pat thought of the lung cancer cases she was studying. Smokers were aware of the risk; they damaged their health knowingly. And she knew as well that offenders were often victims of their environment, or simply of circumstance. It annoyed her that it was a policeman she had to hear this from, but at the same time she was pleasantly surprised by his pattern of thought. "One to nothing," she said. "You know how to defend yourself."

Their stocky elderly waitress was visibly overworked. She registered their order with a tired nod of her head that seemed disapproving, as if she wanted to let her customers know that they were the cause of her exhaustion.

"So, what have you found out?"

"Nothing essential, unfortunately. We put our hopes on your colleagues in forensics, but they haven't been able to come up with anything."

"But there must be something there to find," Pat insisted, doubting him.

"I would have thought so too. Anyway, I wanted to ask you, what does precancerous mean?"

Pat was suddenly attentive. "Götze? Where?"

"The lungs!"

"Aha, his smoking. No one is spared. So he was a perpetrator as well." She explained to Manz that the word meant a change in tissue, from which cancer could develop—it was a preliminary stage, so to speak. While she was talking she remembered Sonder bringing up smoking during their conversation. Hadn't he mentioned Götze by name?

"Lung cancer again," Manz noted. "It came up yesterday as well."

"Yes, I'm doing my dissertation on it," Pat quickly interjected. But she hadn't mentioned that before. And she asked herself why she wanted to deflect the talk from Sonder.

"No, I was thinking of the elderly man in your department. Sonder, yes, that's his name. Poor guy. He told us about his illness."

Pat remembered Sonder's last question, the question of whether it was possible that he had gotten sick in place of a heavy smoker. Had he meant Götze? And he had been satisfied with her answer when she said yes—if only half-heartedly. Did he perhaps . . . ? In a split second she thought of the change in him since Götze had disappeared—no one could have missed it. He had seemed freed from a heavy burden ever since. And then that Saturday evening he had told stories that were brimming with a joy of life. Nonsense! Pat was irritated by her own absurd suspicions. The reason must lie elsewhere. How could Sonder have gotten to the Sihl Valley anyway?

Manz was holding the beer that the waitress had served in the meantime, and was waiting for Pat to clink glasses with him. "What are you thinking about?"

119

"Nothing special." Pat shook her head somewhat too strenuously for Manz to believe her.

"You don't want to tell me?"

Pat touched her glass to Manz's. "No!" she said, resolutely sticking out her chin. Was he questioning her? Was this perhaps the real reason he had wanted to have a beer with her? But even if she assumed that Sonder had something to do with Götze's death—hadn't he also said that he could kill him?—she wouldn't betray him. She wouldn't say a word, and she immediately decided to treat their conversation as a medical confidentiality.

Manz saw how serious her expression was, and the doubt in her eyes. "I have no intention of interrogating you," he assured her, sensing her change of mood. "I'm sorry if I gave that impression."

"It's all right. It's your job, after all." She was disturbed by the distrust she had felt toward Adrian.

"That's not why I'm here. Are you here to find out about the autopsy?"

"No, of course not." Pat knew that she too was curious; it was she who had begun asking the questions.

They both had another beer—the exercise had made them thirsty—and their conversation turned to other things. Both were careful not to allude to Götze again.

When Pat drove off in her old Citroën, a large motorcycle passed her. A Harley Davidson, she guessed correctly. Only then did she recognize Adrian's green shirt and sports bag.

14

Once again Bäni requested Thalmann's presence at a lecture. Even though he was too busy, he was an assistant and had to make himself available.

"I'm still waiting for your answer," Bäni said as soon as they left the clinic.

Thalmann was not surprised that Caesar was repeating his offer of Götze's job. He could have interpreted it as a sign of distrust that Thalmann had not accepted instantly and gratefully. "It seems as though I'm taking advantage of a homicide." Though he knew that Caesar would never be able to comprehend his misgivings, he had to say it.

Bäni reacted almost gruffly, "Oh, come now!" and shook his head reassuringly. "Anyone else would be licking his chops at such an offer."

Caesar was right, of course. Pragmatist that he was, he couldn't see it any other way. Thalmann was aware that he could not keep his chief waiting any longer, and Bäni received his acceptance with obvious satisfaction. Why not right away, his self-satisfied nod seemed to say.

The professor took a few minutes before the lecture to address the students. No one could know that what he was saying had been made easier for him by what he had read in the paper that morning. No valuable clues to Götze's murder had been found, it said. Bäni's confidence had been bolstered considerably by the absence of witnesses at the Sihl. "Even an experienced pathologist like myself can still be shocked by violent death," he said in closing, sounding deeply moved. "It always demonstrates in a drastic way how depraved human nature can be, how irrational human thought, how skewed its values." Afterward he asked the students to rise, in memory of the unfortunate Götze.

Thalmann was surprised at how many more students were present than there had been the week before. It could scarcely be owing to the historical overview of the last lecture, or to the weather—it was still as hot as before. The great interest evident today could be due only to Götze's sudden death. To sensationalism, that was to say. And it took only a few moments for Thalmann to recognize that that day's lecture was no less plagiarized than the preceding one. Caesar was obviously making use of Götze's manuscript. He occasionally even used Götze's expressions, which he had ridiculed surreptitiously before.

Everything went well up to the pathogenesis of arteriosclerosis—the most serious form of vascular disease. At least the students, the best indication, accepted it up till then. But Bäni's insecurity showed when he attempted to draw a diagram. He encountered one problem after another even with the material in his hand. He omitted certain words only to have to reinsert them later, and kept changing the direction of arrows, so that each version simply produced new mistakes. The students didn't appreciate it. There was murmuring, a shuffling of feet, a few loud comments of disapproval creating a disturbance that threatened to get out of hand. A number of students in the back rows packed up their things and left through the rear exit, the envy of those who didn't have the courage to do so.

After Bäni had maneuvered his way through the diagram by the skin of his teeth, he motioned to his assistant to turn on the projector. He was in his element showing slides. He expounded on the images in flowery language, repeatedly displaying the verbal skills that students of years past still were raving about. It appeared he would get through the lecture without difficulty. The mood in the lecture hall had calmed down now that more students—even those in the front rows—had taken advantage of the darkness to disappear, knowing well that slipping away in the darkness was preferable to being seen leaving the classroom.

Bäni acted as if he saw nothing of this, but Thalmann knew that his vanity was painfully taking it all in. When the lights came on again he spoke of the importance of a healthy vascular system—the body's organs functioned fully only with optimal circulation. He mentioned the heart and brain, which were affected particularly adversely by bad circulation. Then Bäni told an anecdote all of his students knew. He told it every year at this point. It was a kind of retroactive revenge on his Latin teacher, whom he described as a stocky, acromegalic type who was feared and hated because of the way he used irregular verbs to play sadistic games. He had encountered him at Bellevue many years later, preaching to the drunks and the streetcars. In his piercing, clear speech the old man was imploring them to honor God with reverence and deep humility. "He had found something more powerful than himself," Bäni said with a pointed smile. "Veins like chalk. I was present at the autopsy."

Even as a student Thalmann had found it inappro-

priate to laugh at the sick in front of students aspiring to
be doctors, and tasteless on top of this for Caesar to call
the ravings of an old man the wisdom of age. And he
was annoyed to find that the story still got laughs. But
Thalmann found that Caesar's game had its pitfalls.
There was an undertone to the students' laughter that
made it unclear exactly at whom they were laughing.

Bäni found it difficult to return to the subject of the
lecture. He was suddenly overcome with fatigue. But he
knew that what was to follow—the treatment of risk
factors—would not be a problem, it was general knowledge. He began with nutrition, mentioned the negative
influence of cholesterol, fulminated against the fact that
medical knowledge was being compromised on this issue
by economic interests, and praised the role of cod-liver
oil in inhibiting the development of arteriosclerosis. "But
anyone who doesn't like cod-liver oil can achieve the
same effect with alcohol, taken in moderate amounts, of
course." And then he added cheerfully, "A bottle of wine
a day is something the liver can tolerate and the vascular
system can demand." But then his smile faded and his
face turned pale and froze like a mask. It was not for
dramatic effect, as many students at first believed. The
wine label with the tower had appeared to him suddenly.
It halted his train of thought, was ineradicable as if etched
in stone. And his flustered attempt to banish the symbol
was unsuccessful. Coughing to cover his embarrassment,
Bäni went over to the water fountain to moisten his forehead and neck with cool water and wash out his mouth.
That helped somewhat. Then he excused himself for his
momentary indisposition, blaming the heat, and was able
slowly to return to the subject. He discussed the effects
of continual stress, high blood pressure, lack of exercise
and heavy smoking. And as he began to wind up the

lecture with his usual tirade against smoking, which he considered idiotic and labeled a protracted attempt at suicide, a familiar face suddenly appeared to him. It looked right at him with a cynical smile, a cigarette dangling from the corner of its mouth. Bäni again began to cough.

"Toss down some rye, the mill is running dry," a student called out disrespectfully. With that, the lecture came to a premature end.

From far away Professor Bäni heard the laughter and the clamor of the classroom emptying. He collapsed onto the nearest chair. Thalmann fought his way through the stream of students to the front of the classroom to come to the aid of his superior.

"Nerves," said Bäni. "Take me home, please."

His collapse made the rounds. Even Häberli heard about it when he called that afternoon. The professor had gone home, Fräulein Stäuble said, he wasn't feeling well.

15

Häberli detested working in dark rooms. He liked to look out the window now and then, to be distracted creatively, as he put it, by the clouds moving by. And even now, with only the vapor trails of an airplane scoring the deep blue sky, he would have preferred bright light to the confining half-darkness of his office had it not been for the sun's merciless heat. He was just letting down the shutters when Manz entered the room.

Häberli sat down at his desk and wiped his forehead with a handkerchief. "This heat again," he groaned. It wasn't even ten yet.

"You said it," Manz agreed. He could not recall ever having seen the commissioner without a tie before.

The room was furnished in a practical, utilitarian style; two walls were covered with gray file cabinets. Several cacti and a landscape, property of the state, provided a personal touch, as well as a large elephant carved of wood that stood on the desk, a gift from a former secretary. Häberli liked to think of it as an affectionate allusion to himself.

"My visit to Professor Rusterholz." Manz handed the commissioner a three-page report that he had typed himself the evening before. Then he sat down across from his boss.

Häberli appreciated his colleague's short and precise reports, he totally trusted Manz's powers of observation and judgment. "Is his alibi for Tuesday credible?" he asked, laying aside the report for the moment.

"It's going to be hard to shake," Manz answered. "According to him he was playing chess from seven to eleven o'clock. With a government counsel. People's Party."

Häberli grinned. They weren't exactly in the same camp politically, but were in complete agreement when it came to the credibility of politicians.

"And they're covering for each other for Wednesday, the two professors," Manz continued. "There's a cook, by the way, an Italian who has worked for him for years. She confirms what he says, of course. She has to."

"So you don't believe them!"

"There's nothing worse than dealing with influential people. They immediately start flexing their muscles, are always friends with some politician or judge, and threaten to ruin your career if you cross them."

"Did Rusterholz say anything to that effect?"

"Not directly, but he clearly insinuated it." And then Manz gave free rein to his anger. "At least with a pimp you can say to his face that you don't believe him, but with these guys you've immediately got a lawsuit to deal with."

"Just don't let yourself be intimidated. Go about your investigation competently and strike at the right moment, without mercy. That's the way to handle these people. They only make themselves suspect when they bring their influence into it, but they don't know that. Anyway, arrogance is a weakness to be exploited."

Manz nodded. Häberli was right, of course. But he couldn't react that calmly, not yet, and he would never be able to see things as innocuously as the commissioner, he thought.

"Anything else?" Häberli tapped the report with his index finger.

"The wine cellar is the only thing there that was satisfying. When I asked Rusterholz if he had a Château Latour, he invited me to follow him. Most impressive, is all I can say. He has the finest châteaux of the Bordelais, the best vintages of the last forty years. And not individual bottles—no, he has them by the dozens. And in addition to the Lafite-Rothschild, the Mouton-Rothschild, the Cheval-Blanc, and all the rest is, of course, the Latour."

"And did he recently give one away?"

"At first he denied it. Then when I mentioned Götze and asked if he had made him a gift of a bottle, he said he had, but that it was months ago and he couldn't remember which wine it was. 'But certainly not a bad one,' he added."

"What do you think?"

"Cleverly thought out, he seems to have covered himself."

"Yes," the commissioner said in contemplation.

"He offered me a bottle, by the way."

"A Château Latour?"

"No. I would have accepted that, as material evidence," Manz laughed. "No, it was a Saint-Emilion, also a good choice, as Rusterholz said. 'You have to start young to enjoy fine wines, in order to savor them as they deserve in old age.' At any rate he said it cleverly enough not to make it sound like a bribe."

When Häberli later intimated that he too had made certain inquiries concerning Rusterholz, the sly look in his eyes betrayed the fact that he had discovered something. He hadn't had to go too far back in the court records before he came across a charge of negligent homicide. Malpractice with fatal consequences. The case had been closed only a few weeks before, and the certification that there was no connection between the medical treatment and the sudden death of the woman in question, which relieved Rusterholz of responsibility, was signed by Bäni.

Manz whistled through his teeth. My respects, he thought, the chief had a good nose. "And that could establish a motive for getting rid of Götze. Blackmail!"

"Possible," the commissioner said, "but highly speculative, you have to admit."

Manz nodded. "But you think those two are up to something as well, don't you?"

"I have learned over the years to suspect almost everyone of almost anything," the commissioner replied, with a smile bordering on sadness.

16

Sonder was surprised when the secretary's office notified him that he still had vacation time coming. He had not expected any after his stay at the sanatorium, and in view of his approaching retirement had not considered vacation time at all. He had two weeks coming to him, they said. So his last day of work would be at the end of the next week. Sonder acted immediately and rescheduled his flight to Tanzania that same day, moving it up two weeks. The woman on the telephone confirmed the change: June 22, 11:40 A.M., Egypt Air from Zurich-Kloten over Cairo to Dar-es-Salaam. A Sunday, two days after his final day at the clinic.

Every single day was important to him now. He wanted to begin his new life as soon as possible. That was the reason for his haste, not because he was afraid they suspected him. No, he wasn't thinking of escape. He was so unconcerned about Götze that anyone who knew the truth would have been astonished. He was aware, of course, that a sudden departure—and his trip could certainly create such an impression—could appear suspicious in the light of the unsolved murder. But he wasn't afraid of being questioned more closely in the matter.

Sonder had made a list of what he needed to take care of during the time left him in Zurich. He had to visit various offices to tend to the technicalities of resettlement. Yes, resettlement—emigration it was called, when you left your homeland after an active life, to go in search of freedom. He was deeply moved by this idea. Once, during the time he had taken up arms as a citizen, he had talked about a free Switzerland. He meant another kind of freedom now, perhaps a freedom he could not have in his own country.

On this Thursday evening he began the most difficult work he had yet before him, that of clearing out his apartment. A lab worker from the clinic had come over with her boyfriend. They had a booth at the flea market each Saturday and were always on the lookout for profitable wares. They brought crates with them, which they were now carting into the building. Sonder led them into the kitchen, where they began packing up the dishes and silverware, the pans, the bread basket, the covered cheese dish, the old scales with the stone weights. Sonder told the young couple to take whatever they thought they could use. Everything had to go, he said; what they didn't take he would throw away. He had put all he needed on the table in the parlor.

"I envy you, simply being able to go away," the young man said.

"I was never anyone to be envied, and I still am not," Sonder remarked, and he handed him a large stoneware cider jug.

"I'm sorry." The young man was embarrassed. He had forgotten what his girlfriend had told him. And Sonder didn't give the impression of being in pain; he was preparing for an adventure, after all, not for his sick bed.

"I'm not leaving because I want to. I'm leaving because I must," Sonder said, immediately adding, "I can't stand it here any longer." He didn't want any misunderstandings.

After they finished in the kitchen they moved on to the other rooms. Sonder gave away without regret objects that had surrounded him for decades. Books, vases, the hand-painted plates with the hunting scenes, porcelain figurines, several woodcuts, the large clock over the buffet, the pictures from the walls. They were all wrapped in newspaper and cloth and packed in crates until the crates were full. Sonder didn't think any of it was valuable. He had set aside his stamp collection and a few engravings to take to a fellow choir member who dealt in such things. He was therefore astonished at the sum the young man, having written everything down, now offered him.

Both of them promised to return again the following week. There were still chests and drawers full of things, and they hadn't even been in the parlor yet. Sonder had not yet been able to decide whether to give away the weapons that hung there. They represented more to him than just memories. They had become something like symbols to him—particularly his hunting rifle, after his battle with the wild boar, and the projectile with which he had recently defended himself—it was hanging in its wire snare as before. He had to separate from them, of course, that was clear, he couldn't take the weapons with him. But he wanted to keep them all together, even if they were packed in a crate in a basement somewhere. He considered these weapons to be his legacy, and thought that one day they would be the only proof that he had existed.

Sonder was not upset by the bare kitchen; on the contrary, even more than his plane ticket, the sight of it assured him that he was leaving and that all this would soon belong to the past. He took food and a beer from the refrigerator, and milk for the cats. He sat outside as he often had over the years. But today he cut his sausage and cheese with a packing knife, and the bread he broke with his hands. He had kept the cats' tin bowl, he wanted to take it with him. A packing knife, a bowl, and a cup, that would be enough.

"You won't miss me, either," Sonder said later without sadness, as the black cat rubbed against his legs.

17

It had been a long time since Sonder had worn his dark suit. Only twice in the last ten years, both times to a funeral. The waistband was a bit tight, but he could tolerate it for a few hours. And what did it matter that it smelled of mothballs, Sonder told himself, as long as it wasn't moth-eaten. He didn't doubt for a moment that this would be the last time he would wear it.

Professor Bäni had stressed the fact yesterday that he expected everyone at the cemetery; he considered it a matter of course, no matter what they thought of Götze. Sonder didn't mind. He had been working for the department for decades doing what was asked of him, and since the funeral was taking place during working hours he saw his attendance as a duty, nothing more, just like his presence at Bäni's birthday party. He didn't feel that this funeral had anything to do with him; he rarely thought of what had happened up at the edge of the forest. He hadn't forgotten that Tuesday, of course—but it seemed a long time ago, much more than the ten days—and he was aware that he had made a large contribution to the cause of present gathering. But he didn't feel responsible. Götze, in his opinion, was the only one to be held responsible.

The few people who had gathered to accompany Horst Götze on his last journey were glad to get out of the glaring sun and into the funeral home. Imelda Stäuble tried in vain to stay cool by fanning herself with her gloved hands. It seemed even hotter than it had been the day before. The majority of those present worked in Pathology. Only one lab worker was missing; she had refused to come, and was prepared to suffer the consequences. A few other physicians were standing around, at least one from each department, as well as the director of the clinic, Dr. Arpagaus, and the head of administration.

A striking woman with a ten-year-old boy was easily recognizable as Frau Bernasconi, Götze's ex-wife. The man who recognized and greeted them, but did not stand with them, looked as if he might be a brother of the deceased. Manz stood off to one side, hoping perhaps not to be noticed, but there were too few people for that. Häberli was correct when he had said there wouldn't be much evidence of grief. It appeared to be a bothersome occasion for everyone, and the weather was doing its part. Professor Bäni was the only one who seemed genuinely moved. Manz could not see Frau Bernasconi's face from where he was standing, it was covered by a black veil, but he knew how she felt about her former husband from their telephone conversation. She had reddish-blond hair that fell below her shoulders, and was tall—she must have been half a head taller than Götze. Her black silk dress was cut loosely, elegant but not suitable for a funeral, Manz felt.

"The police, here! Tactless!" Bäni whispered to Sonder, who was standing next to him. Sonder didn't respond, as they were instructed at that moment to take a seat in the pews at the front.

"Gottfried, the powerless, saw fit to . . ." Sonder thought to himself when he heard the stock phrase used to express God's relation to a human being's death. He had not been to church since God, in his omnipotence, had taken his child from him and then his wife, depressed by the child's death. Nor had he wasted any thought on this God, he had forgotten him with time. But wherever he was in the world he allowed others their God or gods, and respected their saints as well as their demons.

The pastor was speaking now of the deceased, a man he clearly had not known. He kept having to refer to the notes someone else had obviously prepared for him. The funeral speech was sprinkled with clichés employed to gloss over a life that could not exactly be called Christian, to clarify, to justify it. The pastor betrayed some practice at this. In closing, he said that God had allowed an injustice to occur that must be atoned for. The misguided perpetrator would have to answer to God, the pastor announced. No one could escape God's omnipotent retribution.

Pat asked herself if God, or the gods, had not always been needed to make injustice bearable—injustice, at any rate, that was anchored in nature itself. Wasn't a physical disadvantage, whether hereditary or meted out by fate, an inequality that the sick interpreted as an injustice? She thought of her conversation with Göpf Sonder, the one they had held in her office. It was the second time that she had been reminded of it in the context of Götze's death. She had tried to explain to him how it could happen that an illness would strike one person and spare another. Could Sonder have misunderstood her? Had he seen his standing in for Götze, as he had put it at the time, not as a given, but as something that could have been prevented? Had he perhaps even believed that

he could outwit fate? If that were true, then Götze's death
took on a logic that everyone was searching for. But killing him—from this point of view she could not call the
act murder—would be absurd. It benefited no one, Sonder least of all. And if he really had done the deed based
on what she had said, then was she guilty as well, she
asked herself, because she had spoken to him of nature
and not of . . . God's mysterious ways? The pastor was
just mentioning them.

"It is always particularly difficult not to doubt God's
mysterious ways, to doubt them when a beloved person
loses his life at the hands of a sinner."

Pat looked around her and saw the detached expressions on the faces of the others, and the hint of a smile
on Sonder's. Whatever had happened, she didn't think
of herself as a major accomplice.

"We ask you, O Father, to accept him in Your perfect
majesty."

Sonder shook his head imperceptibly.

Bäni had barely listened to the pastor's words. He was
sitting there tensely, nervously, for soon he would have
to deliver his respects. It was expected of him. Following
the principle of "de mortuis nil nisi bonum" he had committed a few lines to paper the day before that were not
in the least ambiguous. And he had read the text aloud
several times to familiarize himself with it. He hadn't
wanted to take the piece of paper with him, it would not
make a good impression, in his opinion. But now he
wished he had it. He felt like a pupil facing his exams,
who suddenly was sure he had forgotten everything he
had learned. Earlier, he had been able to depend totally
on his presence of mind. He had always found the right
words with no trouble, and the right tone as well. In this
situation he would easily have been able to speak extem-

poraneously for half an hour. But those days were gone. He had discovered this painfully two days ago. His bungled lecture had left its mark. He could not endure that kind of a fiasco here, not in front of his department, not in front of Dr. Arpagaus, and especially not in front of the police.

When the pastor finished and nodded to him, Bäni stood up mechanically and walked stiffly to the front. As he stood before the people scattered among the pews and waited for the organ music to end, he felt abandoned. He began, as had the pastor, with "Fellow mourners," but it sounded different coming from his mouth. Bäni himself was shocked at how hollow his voice sounded in this space, how empty, even dead. The platitudes that followed scarcely differed from those of the pastor, until he could no longer avoid speaking of Götze directly.

"In Doctor Götze we have lost a physician who took his profession seriously, who knew that even work done behind the scenes served the ill equally well, who did not tolerate half-measures. He demanded a great deal of himself and of his co-workers in carrying out this exacting work. Everyone who worked with him knows that he always demanded total dedication, but knows also that his own dedication bordered on self-sacrifice. It is with this in mind that we must . . . judge Doctor Götze, if we wish to do him justice in our thoughts."

Though it was a good beginning, Bäni felt unsure of himself, for what he had said scarcely matched his prepared text. He had not intended to heap boundless praise on the deceased. But he found himself in a situation— he had not anticipated Manz being there—where this tactic seemed advisable. He decided to avoid anything problematic, it was his skin, after all. And he figured he would run less risk of a slip of the tongue with praise than with a critical tribute. A rash comment could be disastrous. Bäni looked out over the rows of seats, glancing from face to face and dwelling briefly on Manz's, who was sitting far in the back. Bäni was looking for confirmation, less for what he said than for how he said it, hoping to find it in the hint of a nod. He found no trace of this anywhere. He searched the faces again, and again glanced for a moment at Manz. It passed through Bäni's mind to stop where he was, to close with the comment that it was useless to expend any further words on the deceased. He suppressed the thought with horror.

Just as the situation was becoming painful—several people had begun to look around them cautiously—Bäni roused himself with an embarrassed smile that gave the impression that he was seeking understanding for the pathos he had created.

"Doctor Götze . . . Doctor Horst Götze . . . was taken from us in the midst of prolific productivity, in the midst of a splendid career." Bäni gave a sigh of relief, knowing that once he had gotten hold of a thought the words came of themselves. "He was tireless in his efforts to make new scientific discoveries, and it was important to him as well to pass these on. The large number of articles that originated from his pen is evidence of how involved the deceased was in medical progress."

Pat remembered Caesar's sarcastic comments on how publication-happy his assistant director was, squeezing several articles and lectures out of anything resembling a piece of data. And despite the noble motives that Caesar attributed to Götze, she was not the only one who still saw before her the unrepentant egoist for whom there were interesting cases but never interesting patients, and who in his pathological ambition grabbed at anything, inspired by the belief—or was it, in the end, the knowledge—that it was quantity that advanced a career above all else.

"Doctor Götze's field of action always lay behind the front lines," Bäni continued. "A pathologist does not enjoy the high regard of those colleagues who practice at the bedside or in the operating room, though it is the ill alone whom his demanding work benefits."

When Bäni paused, his eyes again searched the pews and again paused at Manz's face. And it suddenly seemed as if no one were looking at him, they were all looking past him. A chill ran down his spine. The unadorned room, his last words still hanging in the air, the expressionless faces that didn't seem to see him, the coffin behind him with the two wreaths—"Requiescat in Pace" and "Department of Pathology, St. Stephan's Clinic" was printed on one ribbon in gold and black—all of this closed in on Bäni now.

As before, he broke the quiet that again had gone on for too long by clearing his throat, without smiling this time, but again it was puzzling. Imelda Stäuble, who had been sitting stock-still until then, turned around furiously when two lab workers behind her began to giggle.

"Doctor Götze . . . in losing him we have lost a man . . . whom we could always depend on. The most difficult tasks could be given him with confidence. Whoever knew him appreciates—appreciated—that about him. I would like to say that he was a vital support to me as well, a pillar of strength in any situation . . ." Suddenly—the river, the rain, the night when nature had gone wild and threatened to swallow him up. He saw himself clinging to Götze, deathly afraid. A pillar of strength in any situation. The bare walls hurled his words back at him

140

mercilessly, back into his head where they echoed further, bouncing off his concave skull, ever faster, ever harder, ever louder. A pillar of strength in any situation. "May he rest in peace." Bäni tried to shout down the diabolical humming noise, but his voice failed him. The words, though, loud enough that people could understand him, had something beseeching in them, but were most significant in that they seemed to be the first honest ones he had uttered.

With this, his eulogy found an abrupt but not, in anyone's opinion, a premature end. Organ music played solemnly as Bäni strode back to his seat. He walked past where he had been seated before and sat down on one of the rear pews, behind Manz. There he collapsed into himself, sad, feeling that he had been abandoned by his co-workers, betrayed even, lonely for Götze, who, he was convinced, would have assumed even this unpleasant task for him.

Had that really been the right eulogy for Götze? Thalmann doubted it. He could not imagine what Caesar hoped to accomplish with his shallow praise. Those present had known the deceased, after all—most of them only too well. Wouldn't this have been the moment to summon up some understanding of the man? In the end no one is solely responsible for his behavior. Bäni could have placed Götze's excessive arrogance in a societal context, where the only thing that counts is what one achieves, not the means with which one achieves it. Thalmann would have attempted to do that, especially as he viewed it as one's Christian duty, a last service to the dead man.

After a final prayer the pastor sent them out into the glaring sun. The shimmering air over the cemetery melted the colors of the graveside flowers, dissolved the rigid shapes of the crosses. All that was lacking was the theme from *The Good, the Bad, and the Ugly*, Pat thought. She was reminded of a burial scene from the film about the Wild West. She envisioned a villain being laid in his grave. The man who murdered him, a harmless citizen to whom many would have expressed gratitude for his deed, stood unidentified in the crowd. Off to one side was the handsome young sheriff, groping in the dark for the killer. Fortunately.

Sonder was thinking that of all those gathered here he would probably be the next to be buried. The thought did not frighten him. He pictured the reddish-brown African earth, a small cross nailed together with his name on it, misspelled perhaps. What did he care? The grave as well as the cross would be overgrown soon enough. And forgotten. He had often visited cemeteries on his trips, to see how people treated their dead. The last time had been in Venice. When he saw the black funeral boat covered in wreaths, with the two golden lions, he decided to go over to the island that held the cemetery, nothing but the cemetery. The contrast with the city was amazing. Walls standing at right angles to one another, as if designed at a drawing board, all painted white, none of them crumbling as everywhere else. The place seemed created for eternity. The dead were placed in the walls high above the ground—in a city that was built on water. Sonder preferred the decaying earth and jackals digging for carrion, not an unpleasant thought.

Manz kept an eye on Frau Bernasconi. As soon as the ceremony was over and people moved in small groups toward the exit, he followed, in order to speak to her outside the cemetery. She didn't appear surprised; apparently she knew who Manz was even before he introduced himself. The way she lifted the veil from her face was provocative, and probably designed to show that she had nothing to hide. She must have been about thirty-five and at first glance was attractive, with her light green eyes and high cheekbones, her reddish-blond hair and large dark-red mouth. Manz asked himself how Götze could have landed this woman. But at second glance he saw that her face was hard, she wore too much lipstick, and her eyes were cold and calculating despite her smile. She sent the boy on ahead to the car. Then she informed Manz that unfortunately she could tell him nothing more than she already had on the telephone, adding, without being asked, that financially she had gained nothing from her husband's death, nothing at all.

Manz believed this; he had looked into Götze's financial situation in the meantime, and knew as well that Herr Bernasconi was the owner of a prosperous, if shady, credit bureau. After a few more questions concerning Götze's habits and life-style, Manz said good-bye to her.

The tires of the silver Porsche squealed shrilly on the soft asphalt as Frau Bernasconi drove off.

18

When Häberli mentioned that he intended to go for a walk in the Sihl Valley that coming Sunday morning, Manz spontaneously offered to accompany him. Häberli couldn't well refuse, though as a rule he preferred to conduct his on-site meditation, as he liked to refer to this practice, alone. He had discovered many years before that he could concentrate on a crime exceptionally well at the scene where it had occurred, that he received impulses and stimuli there that he did not receive in his study. He could not say why this was so, nor had he ever tried to get to the bottom of this phenomenon; he doubted that there was a rational explanation. For him it was nothing more than an attempt to look at what had happened in an impartial and thorough manner, and the aura surrounding the scene of a crime seemed to help him do this. It was precisely this way of observing things that, in his opinion, had earned him the reputation of possessing an extraordinary nose, a seventh sense even. But despite his successes no one had shown any interest in his method. So he was glad to have Manz accompany him. On their day off, of course; that was understood.

Häberli arrived at the appointed meeting place out-

side Hirzel ten minutes early, and walked along the road
for a stretch. It was not quite eight when the big motorcycle drove up. The commissioner hesitated when Manz
asked whether he would like to cover the short distance
on the bike. He didn't want to admit that he was afraid
to, for Manz had a reputation as a cautious driver. When
Manz repeated his offer he accepted, in order not to of-
fend him, and sat down awkwardly behind him, but he
doubted that this was the right way to approach his Sunday observance.

Häberli explained his method on the steep path down
to the Sihl. On a day like this he was trying, he said, to
dissociate himself from the actual event, trying to separate himself from his relationship to those persons involved, from the opinions he invariably had formed, and
to view everything from another angle, from above, as it
were. But he included himself in this as well, analyzing
the way he had chosen to investigate the crime, and also
the impressions he had formed up to then. This often led
to a change in his perception of events, but it did not
mean that new discoveries would simply fall into his lap.
This method too required a certain amount of planning.
Häberli concluded by saying, "It is no accident that we
are confronting the river first. It may seem unimportant,
but to me it is not insignificant."

As they walked side by side down the shady forest
path, Manz thought about what Häberli had said, judging
it to be a promising introduction. Häberli's remarks had
given him a strange feeling of anticipation, without, however, his being able to imagine what he actually expected.
It was unlikely that the murderer would show up here.

The two men soon reached the stretch of land where
the valley narrowed and the water, foaming and roaring,
dashed against huge blocks of limestone, storming

around them to crash against the rocks further on. Fishermen were trying their luck already in the still green water of protected spots. Farther on, the footpath was carved into the rocks and led through narrow passes and finally through a tunnel so low that Manz, walking behind Häberli in the tight spots, had to duck down to enter it. The valley opened up on the other side of the tunnel and a sunny meadow spread out before them.

"The pasture land of the Sihl," Häberli said, and pointed to a house with wooden benches outside. "We'll take some refreshment there on our way back."

"Whether or not we are successful?"

"Any effective attempt at objective thought can be deemed successful, whether it leads to direct results or not."

Manz nodded. Although he had been working with him for over a year now, the commissioner never ceased to amaze him.

"A premeditated murder has special characteristics that arise from the relationship of the perpetrator to his victim," Häberli began again after a while. "Never forget that murder is a creative process, more creative than birth at any rate, as paradoxical as that may appear at first glance." He explained that the way in which a crime was committed, and particularly the weapon, pointed to the murderer's way of thinking, or to his state of mind. Such connections had to be utilized; they often proved invaluable to the solution of the crime.

Manz was struck by how carefully the commissioner weighed each word. "But we know neither how he was killed nor the motive," he objected.

"You're right there, we don't know much. And it is precisely the motive that will determine our way of looking at it." Häberli explained that with murders involving power, money, or esteem, a simple, almost mathematical thought pattern was called for in solving them. Those kinds of killers were predictable, no matter how clever they thought they were. But when other elements came into play, delusional ideas for example, rather than motives that were subject to instinct, it became much more difficult, for there were no rules to fall back on.

Häberli didn't wish to elaborate further. He was content to let Manz know that what he called meditation was not a type of philosophical observation, but rather an attempt to bring the events being investigated in line with the logic of human behavior—which operated on various levels.

They left the path when it diverged from the river to follow the mountain, and continued along the river bank. The low water level made this considerably easier. They proceeded slowly now, as Häberli was very careful climbing over the rocks. To Manz he didn't seem quite sure on his feet, particularly along the ledges that dropped down to the river in places. But the commissioner emphatically rejected his offer of help. If he were here alone he would have to make it by himself, he said. Fearing that he would slip and fall, there was nothing left for Manz to do but follow close behind him, ready to reach out and catch him.

Häberli halted at the place where the fisherman had discovered the body. He stood for a long time looking into the Sihl, whose water this morning flowed quietly and harmlessly. Actually, on this Sunday morning the place was better suited to more tranquil thoughts, he told himself, than those of violent crime.

To the relief of both men, they returned to the path a short while later, and from there it wasn't far to the Hirschfels, the destination of their excursion. It must have been here that Götze's body was put in the water, Manz thought. And on Wednesday evening at the earliest, for sure. It was too open a spot, it would have been impossible for a corpse to lie here on the bank for an entire day without having been seen. Particularly on a nice day—there were too many hikers and too many dogs. The body was probably thrown into the basin under that rock over there. The water was easy to reach from there, even with a car.

Having arrived at the Hirschfels, Häberli sat down on a bench. Manz walked on a little farther, only in part because he didn't want to disturb the commissioner. The place itself held a particular attraction for him. He looked at the rocks—the water was only barely covering them today—and at the basin beyond them; he walked back and forth to view the scene from various angles. This landscape seemed somehow familiar to him, but not from the investigation—he had been to this area for the first time only a week ago. No, he must have seen it somewhere else recently, in some other form. He tried hard to remember, but couldn't. Or had he only dreamed it? No, he was sure that the feeling—and at the moment it was nothing more—was based in reality, a faint memory.

Manz sat down now and tried to concentrate solely on the landscape. He closed his eyes just enough that forms began to blur and colors to fade into one another. He felt he was getting closer to what he was searching for, and when he added the white foam of water plunging over rocks he suddenly knew that it was a picture, a painting, that he had seen recently, accidently, in passing. He excitedly pictured all the rooms he could possibly have been in during the last few days, from Götze's apartment to the rooms of the clinic to Rusterholz's country house. Suddenly Manz leapt up. He had found what he was looking for. At Rusterholz's. A painting on the long wall of the library. One picture among many. He immediately wanted to inform Häberli of his finding, but Häberli was sitting on his bench so calmly, so totally absorbed, with his eyes closed, it appeared, that Manz didn't wish to disturb him. There was time.

But what was it about the picture that had attracted his attention? Manz sat down again and thought about the wall covered with paintings. He squinted as he had before. It couldn't have been the subject, nor the colors. The picture was nice, but really rather unremarkable. There was something about it, though, that didn't fit, something that disturbed the harmony. It was the over-sized signature in the bottom right corner! It was out of place, arrogant; from its corner position it destroyed the feeling of calm that suffused the landscape. It had been an unusual name as well . . . "Caesar." Yes, Caesar was the word written there. And Caesar was Bäni. Pat had used the name. Manz leaned back in satisfaction. Häberli would be surprised.

When the commissioner went over to Manz after an hour of meditation he did not give the impression of having learned anything. He shrugged his shoulders wordlessly and sat down next to Manz on the bench. "The place doesn't give off anything, perhaps because it's not where the crime was committed, who knows. After all, what happened between perpetrator and victim didn't happen here." Häberli said this as if he owed him an explanation.

Manz said nothing. No response was called for.

"How do we know if the murderer was even here?" Häberli added after a while.

"What do you mean?" Manz asked quickly.

"Just a thought."

149

Manz didn't pursue it. He saw this as the moment to report his discovery. And he tried to communicate to the commissioner exactly what it was that had made him think of the painting, where it was hanging, and about the signature. Häberli listened quietly, to Manz disappointingly so.

"Congratulations! You were more successful than I," Häberli complimented him when Manz had finished. "Your gift of observation is extraordinary, an important prerequisite for a career in police work."

"So Bäni must be familiar with this place, at least," Manz said pointedly. He couldn't understand why Häberli was taking the news so calmly.

"Rusterholz rented a fishing spot on the Sihl until five years ago," the commissioner remarked drily. "I was at the Fisheries Inspectorate yesterday and took a look at their books."

Manz looked at Häberli in astonishment. Why had his superior kept this from him?

Häberli took a notebook and pencil from his breast pocket and drew three small circles on a piece of paper with a name next to each. Götze, Bäni, Rusterholz. "Götze's car was parked in front of Bäni's house, the wine came from Rusterholz, and Rusterholz provided Bäni with an alibi," he said, connecting the three circles to one another. Then he drew a circle outside the other three and wrote "Sihl" next to it. "Götze was found here," he said, "Bäni painted here, and Rusterholz fished here," and he extended the lines to form a cone. He tore the paper from the notebook and handed it to Manz. "Normally, that's enough. But this figure is left hanging."

What did Häberli mean by that? By what mental process had he arrived at it? Manz remained seated when the commissioner got up to leave. Häberli owed him an explanation, he thought, here and now. Did he know more than he was saying? Only when Häberli turned to go did Manz stand up.

"If you look at Götze's case closely, it's clear that something is odd," Häberli began unasked, as Manz joined him. "It seems to be a perfect crime. No clues, no witnesses, no clear motive. But suddenly there's one indication after another, and they all point to the professors, make them suspect. That's what puzzles me. It smells like a trap. Whether it was set deliberately or not, I don't know. Not yet."

"And the professors didn't have anything to do with it?"

"I didn't say that. I just don't believe the solution lies with them alone. It seems to me that they're caught in the trap somehow, and at the same time they're the bait that's supposed to lure us in."

Manz, who an hour before had been sure that he had discovered an essential clue, didn't know what to say to this unexpected statement. He didn't dare dismiss it as a crazy notion; Häberli's ideas had proven correct too often for that. And yet what Häberli was suggesting sounded fantastic. Manz needed time to think about it, to digest the crumb he had been tossed.

Häberli hesitated briefly at the place where the path left the Sihl, to consider whether he wanted to scramble over the rocks again. For the sake of consistency he had to, had to follow the path the corpse had taken. Under the circumstances, however—that was to say, after the rather fruitless exercise so far—he decided that the additional effort was unnecessary. On top of which, he was afraid to continue along the river in the glaring sun.

151

FELIX METTLER

Manz, who would not have been surprised had his superior undertaken the strenuous walk a second time, was relieved at the decision.

The long silence between the two men was broken by the robust greeting of a man walking a long-haired sheepdog on a leash. He was reminded, Häberli said, of a case he had read about in an English journal, *The Criminologist*, a case that had taken place in France years ago. An industrialist had been murdered, and all the evidence pointed to two arms dealers, who had been visiting the man at the time, as the perpetrators. It all seemed obvious—in their line of business there was no dearth of motives—but the two men got away and were nowhere to be found. As a result, the investigation was dropped. But years later came a confession from another source entirely, contained in the will of a former employee of the murdered man. He had been terribly deceived, it stated. He had believed that he was producing weapons parts for the French army, the director had assured him of this, and then he had discovered quite by accident that the parts were being delivered to the police of a Central American dictatorship. Staunch socialist that he was, he had seen no other way to make amends than to kill the director who had deceived him. So the arms dealers, suspect in any case because of their vocation, apparently had only hidden the body, to gain time to escape. "How could the murder have been connected to the little freedom fighter, far removed from events, who had acted to regain his honor?"

"A perfect murder in the end," Manz remarked, "though scarcely planned as such."

"That's right. Though I doubt that one can plan the perfect crime. Nothing is totally foreseeable. No, no. Even the most insignificant coincidence can wreck the

152

shrewdest scheme, and make the cleverest of fellows look like a fool. There is plenty of evidence of that. But the opposite can apply as well. One fortunate encounter can suffice, or an unfortunate one, I should say, and a simple act becomes so obscure, so illogical, that its circumstances are scarcely to be determined. And so a simple murder can in the end become a perfect crime. As in the case of the factory director in France—and who knows, perhaps in our case as well."

Before he was even seated at the Sihlmätteli restaurant Häberli ordered a half bottle of Räuschling and two glasses, without asking Manz what he would like to drink. He wiped his face and bald head with his handkerchief before he lowered himself onto a wooden bench with a loud sign of relief.

"More refreshing than a Latour," Häberli laughed, after taking a big swallow of the cool white wine.

"And lighter!"

"Yes, and lighter. By the way, is Bäni a good painter?"

Manz was surprised by the question. He was pleased that Häberli was giving some weight to his discovery. "I couldn't be the judge of that. But I recognized the landscape, that's something," he laughed.

"Keep at it, in any case. But don't get too near the professors. At this moment the path to our goal most likely cuts through them. For the time being I see no other way."

Manz smiled in amusement. Häberli's enjoyment of the cool wine had apparently led him back to reality.

19

Häberli regularly lunched at a restaurant not far from headquarters. He usually ate alone and he always sat at the same table, somewhat off to one side. The restaurant wasn't fancy; it could just as well have been located somewhere in the country. A portrait of a dark-eyed gypsy woman hung over his table, across from an old ox yoke, and up front, near a glass case with the flag and the pewter mugs of a riflemen's association, was a photograph of the General. After four decades, it was still there.

As a rule Häberli ordered one of the two specials, hearty, plain fare prepared by the proprietress herself. He drank mineral water, occasionally a beer. It was here that he read the daily paper. The local news, and the national and international political news, in that order. He scanned the sports and culture sections and set aside the financial section. And for weeks he had been following the weather forecast closely, which he ordinarily barely paid attention to, though lately it seemed only to repeat itself. Häberli valued this midday interruption; it allowed him some distance from his work. There were no policemen here, nor criminals, nor even suspects. These were totally normal people whose weaknesses might, at worst, cause them to have a brush with the law at some point in their lives. Drunk driving, petty fraud, the failure to pay a bill, perhaps, or pilfering the club's treasury, nothing that Häberli was interested in as long as it wasn't connected to an assault on life or limb.

It was Monday. As far as Götze's case went, it had been an unproductive morning. Häberli had set all his hopes on forensics, and they had given him nothing more than a regretful shrug of the shoulders. He could understand the regret. To be unable to ascertain a cause of death would gnaw at an expert's pride. He himself was troubled when the solution to a murder was slow in coming. Nothing new concerning Götze's whereabouts that Tuesday evening had come in over the weekend. So when he left the restaurant after coffee, Häberli could not have known that he was about to get precisely this information. He would not have guessed that the delicate Asian woman hesitating in front of the gate—he was not the only one to notice her—was about to deliver this important piece of news. He had barely closed the door to his office when the telephone rang and a visitor was announced. A Miss Tuong—the name immediately made Häberli think of the girl standing in front of the building. He called Manz in right away.

Häberli lined up two chairs. He didn't sit behind his desk, as was customary when taking statements, but in front of it, directly across from Miss Tuong. Manz placed his chair to one side a short distance away.

"What is it you wish to tell us?" Häberli began, when everyone was seated.

The young woman, who had said nothing up to that point, remained silent as well at this question. She seemed intimidated, which surprised Manz, for the commissioner had taken an almost fatherly tone with her.

And he himself would have said she was a child. The wide-spaced eyes, the flat nose, the small mouth, all awakened his protective instincts.

"You knew Doctor Horst Götze, that's true, isn't it?" the commissioner ventured.

Her dark eyes widened briefly when he uttered the name, then she nodded.

"And you saw him on Tuesday?"

Her "yes" sounded like a bird's chirping.

"In the evening?"

She nodded again. Häberli gave Manz a meaningful look.

"Tell us, please, where you saw him and when, exactly."

"At the Elvira Salon," she said with a shy smile, "that evening at seven." She had a high voice and a strong accent.

As they talked further and she became more relaxed, she revealed that Götze visited her every other Tuesday at the Elvira Salon, a massage parlor in the Fourth District, that he always arrived at seven and spent a good half hour with her. On his last visit he had stayed somewhat longer, she said. Ten minutes perhaps, no more. And with downcast eyes she revealed to the commissioner, who was pushing her for more exact information, that Doctor Horst, as she called him, sometimes needed a little extra time to relax. But Häberli wasn't interested in that. He only wanted to know the exact time that Götze had left the salon and what physical shape he had been in. It could not have been later than a quarter to eight, Miss Tuong finally stated; Doctor Horst never made any trouble, and had left that evening as usual. As to where Götze usually parked his car and whether he went to any particular bar or restaurant after his visit, she didn't know. He talked very little about himself, she said, and had not mentioned to her that he was intending to go to a party.

When in closing Häberli asked why she had not come in before, she answered that she had not known about it before. She had seen a picture of Doctor Horst in the newspaper the day before by accident, it was the first she had learned of what had happened. Someone had told her about it. And she had come because she wanted to avoid trouble with the police.

The article she mentioned, which had appeared in a gossip sheet, had been sent to Häberli that morning through the departmental mail—by a colleague, he assumed; there was no salutation or note attached. It was certainly no journalistic masterpiece, more a polemic that chastised the police for their investigation into Götze's murder. It appeared that the writer, a hack who apparently had trouble enough doing his job, was taking the case in his own hands. Häberli was amused, he was used to this sort of thing by now.

No sooner had the young woman left the room with Häberli, who insisted on escorting her to the exit, than Manz grabbed the phone and ordered someone to tail her until she returned to her salon.

Häberli nodded when Manz informed him of this measure. "It's warranted."

"I see no reason to doubt the girl's story," Manz said. It wasn't hard to read the commissioner's mind. "If she had anything to do with the murder she would have avoided drawing attention to herself. But for the record it's better she did. Actually, we should check with Vice on the Elvira Salon."

Häberli agreed. "So that was the appointment our Doctor Götze had," he smiled, shaking his head.

157

They both had to admit that they had expected more of Götze's whereabouts on that evening. The lone locale where he had spent the time in question cast a new light on things; a visit to such an establishment was better kept quiet. If the girl's statement was true, they reflected, then Götze must still have intended to go to the party after leaving the salon. So now they had to find out what had happened immediately afterward that could have kept Götze from carrying out this intention. And then they narrowed it to the likelihood that the killer knew of one or the other of Götze's engagements. They agreed that any other version would call for too great a coincidence.

"You said recently that you'd rather deal with pimps than with professors. Well, then!" Häberli would have been sorry had their investigation led them away from the clinic into the Zurich demimonde.

But there was the matter of the victim's car parked in front of Bäni's house, and it pointed to the fact, Manz said, that the gloved driver, the killer in all probability, knew of Götze's professional relationships. A point well taken. The twists and turns of the case always led them back to Götze's medical milieu, with the St. Stephan's Clinic at its center. There, they agreed, the key to the puzzle must lie.

Manz nodded in agreement when Häberli suggested paying the clinic another visit the following day. The case had kept him awake the night before. Since his walk along the Sihl he had not been able to shake his suspicion that the two professors were involved in this. On the contrary, like someone struggling with a brain twister, he had followed this thought wherever it had led him. This morning as well. But no matter how he approached it, there remained things of which he could make neither rhyme nor reason. The location of the car was a major one. So with Häberli's suggestion he was thinking more of a confrontation with Professor Bäni, whom he intended to ask a few pointed questions, than of Pat. He hoped to run into her that evening at the health club.

Häberli remarked that they should extend their investigation to other departments as well, as everyone in Pathology had an alibi for the evening in question. The alibis! They had all been at the party, all but one. It suddenly occurred to Manz that Sonder would have traveled through the section of town in which the Elvira Salon was located on his way from the train station to the soccer stadium.

"As far as I recall, it would have been impossible for the two of them to have encountered each other there." The commissioner leafed through his file. "Here! Sonder was at the train station at a quarter after seven, someone spotted him. So he was on his way there at a time when Götze was already at the salon."

"The car! Sonder could have seen the parked car from the tram. It was obvious enough . . ."

"Which prompted him to commit an unpremeditated murder?" Häberli interrupted, looking at Manz questioningly.

"Why not? He hated him, like everyone else."

"Because the murder wasn't unpremeditated," Häberli said, shaking his head. "There's too much evidence against that."

"At any rate, Sonder would have had plenty of time if he weren't at the game," Manz said, trying to spin out the thread. "He wasn't seen again until after the game was over."

Häberli nodded. He had to agree with his colleague on this. "But hate alone is not motive enough, nor is revenge, not with this man," he objected. "Besides, as

159

far as I know, Sonder doesn't own a car. How would he have gotten the body to the Sihl?"

"Maybe he had accomplices."

The commissioner laughed softly. He knew what was firing Manz up. The flicker in his eyes was enough to give it away. Häberli had long since known how gladly Manz would have pinned something on the two professors. "I don't know Sonder well," he said, laughing mildly, "but I would judge him to be a loner."

"Fine," Manz waved him off. He had to admit that Götze's car parked at Bäni's house had once again thwarted his theory. "It's probably unimportant," he added.

"But you can check Sonder's alibi, of course." Manz needed a little encouragement. And Häberli would have been the last person to restrain a colleague's imagination.

20

Häberli and Manz drove to St. Stephan's Clinic early that Tuesday afternoon. Frau Moosbacher admitted them without the usual appointment. At the director's orders, she said.

Doors stood open everywhere, and the offices were in semidarkness, in an attempt to relieve the debilitating heat in any way possible. Now she looks like a scientist, Manz thought, as he saw Pat sitting at the microscope, glasses on the top of her head. Thalmann was there as well, sitting at his desk, writing and leafing through a book simultaneously. Manz had hesitated for a moment when Häberli had instructed him to visit Pat Wyss first and then Sonder, but he did as he was told. The commissioner obviously wanted to drop in on the professor himself.

Manz cleared his throat as he entered the room, said hello, and asked if he could disturb them. Thalmann seemed obliging as he stood up and immediately assured Manz that he was not intruding. After all, the reason he was there concerned them as well, he added. In contrast, Pat greeted him rather coolly—at least it appeared so to Manz, which again made him suspect that her reticence of late had to do with his job after all. But why? Surely she had nothing to fear? Or had she?

They chatted for a while, first about the heat—under the circumstances the weather was a legitimate topic—then about the additional workload to be dealt with since Götze's death. Pat was now working full time. She would have to put off her dissertation for the moment, she said. That turned the subject to Götze's death. Manz directed his first question to Thalmann. "Did you know that Doctor Götze planned to arrive somewhat late that Tuesday?"

"I only found that out at the party, when he didn't come," Thalmann answered. "No, I didn't know it beforehand."

Manz nodded and turned to Pat. "Did anyone besides you know that Doctor Götze would not arrive until after eight?"

"I scarcely think Götze made a secret of it," Pat answered. "I didn't mention it to anyone, however. There was no reason to."

"Are you sure? Think again who else might have known," Manz persisted. "It could be important to us."

"Yes, I'm sure," Pat said decisively, and looked him in the eyes almost defiantly. She knew, of course, that Sonder had been present when Götze mentioned his appointment. But she didn't want to admit it. And she already had worked out a justification for her denial, a legitimate one that went beyond her personal feelings. Pat had concluded that understanding the nature of illness was very rare, even among her colleagues, to say nothing of judges. There was no question, she told herself, that a person who committed a crime was likely to receive a milder sentence were it discovered that he had had an operation for a brain tumor. Anyone would agree that abnormal behavior was easily explicable by possible brain damage. But no one would accept the same argument for a person with a lung tumor, though experts knew that even the slightest metabolic change could affect behavior. Depression, changes in perception too, could be traced back in part to abnormal enzymes. And malignant cancer cells have a different metabolism. But who considered that? Who could say with certainty that psychic disturbances couldn't be traced back to that? *In dubio pro reo!* So a general lack of knowledge concerning the connections between things justified her silence.

"Doctor Götze was seen in town around a quarter to eight." Let the two of them figure out the significance of that, Manz thought to himself, and continued with questions that had to do primarily with Götze's relationship to colleagues in other departments. Their answers weren't very helpful. Yet again! It seemed that no one was particularly interested in Götze the man.

As Manz was saying good-bye to Thalmann he pointed to the photographs over the desk. "This is your work, isn't it?" he asked, and Thalmann answered yes. "I like them. They're really good." And to Pat he said, "See you tonight."

"I don't know if I'm going today. Probably not."

Manz had seen her sports bag near her desk, hence his remark, which he now regretted. She was avoiding him, there could be no doubt about it. But why? He was only doing his job, she must understand that. She couldn't have hated Götze to the extent that his questions alone were the reason for her unfriendliness. Yes, he was interested. Pat herself had given him reason to be. Or had he really been so mistaken about her?

When he reached the doorway Manz turned to ask if Sonder was in the building, and where he could be found. Thalmann answered that he was probably in the library.

Pat felt the blood rush to her head. She was afraid Adrian had noticed her jump at his question.

Only shortly before, Professor Bäni also had hoped that he had not reacted too strongly when the commissioner informed him that a witness had seen Götze in the city after seven-thirty. Häberli told him where the information had come from, but at the same time asked for his discretion, in order not to damage Götze's reputation unnecessarily. Bäni assured him of this, but as soon as the door had closed behind the commissioner he rushed to the telephone. When the secretary announced that Professor Rusterholz was in the operating room and would not be back before three o'clock, Bäni was forced to savor the news alone. The longer he thought about it, the more his feeling of great relief at being certain that he had not killed Götze was mixed with anger. Wasn't it apparent, the way things stood, that he was the intended victim of a malicious plot? And was it, in the end, perhaps even his own colleagues who were out to get him, who had unloaded Götze's body on him? Thereby getting rid of both of them, the director and his assistant, with one fell stroke. The department would then fall into the blackguards' lap like a piece of ripe fruit. Bäni believed he knew his colleagues, believed those of them obsessed with their careers to be capable of almost any unscrupulous act that would help them attain their goal. And at the moment he was none too sure whether, given his action at the Sihl, he had fallen into his enemies' trap or, on the contrary, thwarted their pernicious plans. In the end, only the police investigation would decide. For if he succeeded in concealing his involvement in the case, then the diabolical plan against him had failed. On the other hand, if what had happened two weeks before on the Sihl became known, he was ambushed as intended.

Not exactly as Götze had been, but ambushed nevertheless, perhaps even more cruelly.

Rusterholz, whom Bäni reached in his office on the fourth try, talked his friend out of his wild hunches—as he called Bäni's conjectures—and persuaded him to come to a little celebration the following evening."If we can't celebrate this news, then I don't know what we can celebrate," he said impatiently when his friend hesitated. Bäni's distrust concerning his careerist colleagues had not yet died down.

When Manz entered the library he found Häberli in animated conversation with Sonder. Sonder was leaning against a shelf, talking about himself in earlier times, and Häberli, propped on a window sill, asked a question now and then—straightforwardly, it appeared to Manz —that had nothing at all to do with Götze. Manz browsed in the shelves, noting book titles, as he obviously had some time to spare, whereupon it occurred to him that Pat would understand what was written here. At the same time, he followed the conversation and noted that the two men were entertaining each other.

Judging from the way in which the commissioner indicated that he was to take over the conversation, Manz decided that Sonder had not yet been informed of the news. So he told him, explaining why they were there and why they had to go over each person's alibi for the period from 7:30 to 10:00 P.M.

Sonder listened silently, seemingly unimpressed. He answered Manz's questions on the game—Manz had been filled in on it by a colleague who was a sports fan —with convincing composure. Sonder, who had seen a tape of the game on television late that same night, knew that the police band had played before the starting whistle as well as at halftime. Only the question about the color

165

of the majorettes' uniforms irritated him. Though he had no idea of the answer he acted as if he were thinking about it. He quickly considered red or blue, silver perhaps, but to venture a guess would be dangerous. He could get away with saying he didn't remember. After all, at his age one forgot things. Better to forget something like the majorettes, at any rate, than who had kicked the penalty goal, which he was questioned on as well.

"I didn't see any majorettes," Sonder said, without really wanting to. And to his astonishment, Manz nodded.

The commissioner, surprised by Manz's questions, nodded in turn, if for a different reason. He didn't want Sonder to get in trouble. And he thought that it was out of the question that Sonder had had anything to do with this crime.

Häberli credited it less to accident than to a selective curiosity formed over years as a criminologist that he happened to read a handwritten notice posted on the bulletin board as he was leaving the department. It was an invitation to cake and coffee for the coming Friday, on the occasion of Gottfried Sonder's last day at work. The invitation was signed by Pat Wyss. Häberli had assumed that Sonder still had two weeks of work left—until the end of the month.

21

At the heavy wooden doors to "Valhalla"—as Rusterholz called his country home—the two professors fell into each other's arms, slapping each other on the back for a long time, like two Russian brothers who hadn't seen each other for years. Bäni was relieved to have his doubts banished, and even more so not to have to fear punishment for the deed, and the embrace of his friend who had stood by him selflessly during this difficult time brought tears to his eyes—something that had not happened for a long, long time. He would have liked to include in the embrace the little Asian woman Häberli had told him about. What he felt for her was more than gratitude. It was a feeling he couldn't quite put his finger on, but which, he believed, could be expressed by no other word than "love." It had occurred to him to seek out the girl and find a way to show his gratitude.

"God, I'm relieved," he groaned. "You cannot imagine how happy that girl, whoever she is, has made me."

"That's what call girls are for," Rusterholz said sardonically, after he had released his friend from his grasp. He was relieved too, of course, that Caesar had been eliminated as the murderer and he was freed of the burden of responsibility. If this feeling was mixed with a trace of disappointment, however, it was only because he was a gambler through and through. It was as if someone had switched his chess pieces during a game and told him it had been a rook or a knight he had been defending instead of a king. If there was no glory to be had in this game, then at least he would have liked to follow through with his plan and see his brilliant ideas confirmed.

"I could have saved myself the trouble," Bäni murmured, shaking his head, as they passed through the vestibule.

"That's right, damn it," Rusterholz agreed. "That whoremaster got you in a jam. He was being serviced in a massage parlor while you were sleeping peacefully in your bed."

Bäni's laugh had something pained about it. He felt that some of the sarcasm was directed at him.

"And then he didn't want to pay," Rusterholz continued as they ascended the broad stairs side by side, "and was killed by her pimp and thrown in your car."

"No," Bäni countered and stopped, his hand on the banister. "He left as usual, around a quarter to eight, the girl has witnesses to prove it."

"Come on, Caesar, you know that crowd. They lie like dogs. It's utterly ridiculous that the police bought her story."

"I don't know," Bäni said, somewhat offended. "But anyway, it lets me off the hook." He didn't like the way Wotan was talking about the girl. "And she scarcely would have gone to the police voluntarily, to tell a bunch of lies."

"All right, fine," Rusterholz appeased his friend. He knew that he had spoken without thinking. His anticipation of the forthcoming meal had made him brash. He had a premonition of what they could expect. That morning he had heard Maria talking to the pans or to the fire—at her request he had had a wood-burning stove installed. He liked to imagine her as an alchemist reciting magic spells as she prepared her sauces over the fire, sprinkling in her herbs. Anyway, it was a good sign when she talked to herself in the kitchen, it guaranteed something unique. And for this evening he had incited Maria to demonstrate the extent of her talent by promising her an additional week of vacation in her beloved homeland—Tuscany—should he be overwhelmed by her creative cuisine. As generous as this offer appeared—she would be irreplaceable to him during this period—it was in no way selfless. Rusterholz understood the influence that an inspiring landscape exercised over an artist's creativity, and it was he himself who benefited from it.

Rusterholz cheerfully took the lead, stepping out onto the large balcony where he exuberantly switched to a different version. "Maybe Götze's heart gave out. It happens all the time when screwing." He then enthusiastically related the story of the dead cardinal who was carried out of a bordello in Paris and put in the hallway of the building next door. The truth came out only because His Excellency wasn't dressed correctly. This story, which had made the rounds of the papers years ago, pleased him. "It would have been possible, wouldn't it? What do you pathologists see when you look at a heart after a respiratory block or a heart flutter? Nothing, right? And what did Götze's autopsy show? Nothing either. There you have it!"

"And you mean to tell me that they then drove out to my place, at Götze's wish perhaps, where they managed to open the garage in some mysterious way, and toss the body into my car and a bottle of wine into Götze's?" Bäni asked, annoyed. He found the situation too serious to be amused by Wotan's scurrilous notions.

Rusterholz didn't answer, merely shrugged his shoulders and went back into the house. Bäni, lost in thought, stared out into the thick woods that almost totally surrounded the house. So he didn't notice Rusterholz return with a full carafe in his left hand and an empty bottle of Château Latour 1959 in his right, and jumped when he heard Wotan's loud voice behind him.

"It's all nonsense. Now I have it. Götze, of course, drove out to the cabin, and everything happened there. You yourself drove the body home and the sly dog parked Götze's car in front of your house. That's the way it happened, it must have."

Bäni looked at his friend in amazement. Wotan was not joking now, that was clear. "Do you think so? That would be . . ."

"Maybe he even calculated your reaction, Caesar, and created an alibi for himself. If that's true, if it really was planned that way, then I'd like to meet this fellow, even if it means cooperating with the police."

"For God's sake, not that," Bäni called out, horrified. "Then I'm finished—and you too, Wotan, think about it, our alibi."

Rusterholz waved away the thought. "Do you really think I'd do that?" He put the wine on the marble table that stood on the balcony and went back into the house for glasses. Naturally it was clear to him that he couldn't say anything to the police, but he had just realized what an embarrassment it could be to him and Caesar if the perpetrator were arrested. A full confession, which they would have to reckon with sooner or later, would look bad for the two of them. Caesar would be caught in his own trap and would have to admit what he had done with the body, and then he too would be in for it. The

figures on the chessboard had shifted again, and Rusterholz determined with a certain satisfaction that the
game would continue as it had started, even if he were
playing against someone unknown—the murderer.

"But let's turn to the more pleasant side of life," Rusterholz said, reappearing on the balcony with two glasses
in his hand. After pouring carefully, he handed Bäni a
glass. "Today's choice is a given, of course."

"To your health, Wotan," Bäni said.

"To your innocence, Caesar."

They evaluated the wine respectfully, discussed its
depth, sniffed it with their eyes closed, and praised its
full-bodied bouquet. Then they tasted it in little sips,
rolling it around on their tongues and gums, inhaling it,
to locate its inner essence. They declared it to have weight
and force and concentration, and were unrestrained in
vividly describing their feelings.

"It has muscle and mettle," Bäni offered.

"A long-ripened spirit harmoniously combined with
a robust body," Rusterholz pontificated.

But Bäni could indulge himself for only so long, forgetting what a fateful role this wine had played, before
he recalled again the worst day of his life. Wotan's last
version really did have something to it. If he accepted
the idea that the body had been put into his car in the
woods, several riddles that had puzzled him for a long
time were now indeed answered. The possibility that he
could resolve further questions, and maybe even the case,
would not let him be; it forced him to review everything
in a new light. "The murderer either followed him to the
woods, or was waiting for him there," Bäni said, thinking
out loud.

"If it was only one person, then he was waiting for
him," Rusterholz immediately declared. "Then he drove

off in Götze's car and parked it in front of your house."

"Right. Otherwise there would have been at least two of them."

"You have to figure out who would benefit from Götze's death."

"Everyone but me!"

Rusterholz laughed. "Poor unloved Götze!"

"It must have been a colleague," Bäni said. "Why not someone who wanted the position at the university?"

"It wouldn't be the first time a scientific career was launched that way," Rusterholz said with a contemptuous snort, and took another sip of wine.

"For his career a pathologist will walk over dead bodies."

Rusterholz choked, and coughed till he shook. Bäni took the glass out of his hand—the wine was sloshing out of it—and pounded his friend hard on the back.

"You idiot," Rusterholz said in a harsh voice, tears running down his face. "Never say anything like that again while I'm drinking."

Bäni relished this reaction to his bon mot. "Yes, yes, it's the anecdotes that reveal a scholar's spirit," he mused. "Too bad that they're usually either forgotten or attributed to someone else." He knew how greatly anecdotes contributed to a scientist's reputation, and how little, in contrast, the books he wrote did.

"Just hope that it isn't repeated in context," Rusterholz scoffed. He did not appreciate his friend's arrogance.

In the meantime, unnoticed by either of them, almost like a shadow, Maria had appeared on the terrace and placed a platter on the table. "Un mazzetto di fiori," Rusterholz cried at the discovery, in the voice of a circus master, proud of his artistes, announcing the next act.

172

The first, in this case. In addition to prosciutto, slices of salami and salsicce had been shaped into flowers, with olives and strips of peppers. "A rustic note, it perfectly suits my taste," Rusterholz said with delight. And after he had devoured one of Maria's crostini, a bread she baked and then spread with a coarse liver pate, he raved about the unique qualities to be found even in this simple peasant dish. Naive art, so to speak. He could imagine that a Chianti would go well with it, one that was a bit new and undomesticated, but the choice of wine for that day, as he had said, had been a given, and no Château Latour had ever spoiled a meal.

When the dull sound of a gong summoned them to dinner a good half hour later, the men rose immediately, both in excellent spirits—Bäni, because he was convinced that he had not killed the assistant director he had thrown in the river, and Rusterholz, because he was enormously looking forward to the meal. They entered the wood-paneled dining room, so huge that it seemed to Bäni like a museum. Against one wall was a stand covered with old pewter, and there were copperplate engravings and etchings everywhere, all from the region around Lake Zurich. Bäni walked around the table, perfectly proportioned to the room, and took his usual seat. The place settings, though arranged directly across from each other on the two long sides of the table, were a good six feet apart. Before sitting down Rusterholz took the next carafe—there were six standing within reach, each with its own bottle—and decanted the wine.

"To your cook Maria," Bäni said, raising his glass.

"To the cook of all cooks," Rusterholz amended, "to her who rules the most noble of my senses."

Maria entered the room dressed in black, carrying a

173

tray on which were two plates covered with silver lids.

"Ravioli," Rusterholz said, as Maria lifted the lids, and he asked expectantly, "Come si chiama?"

"Misteriosi!" Maria hurried back to the kitchen without another word.

The lord of the manor's face revealed excitement and pleasure, he glowed with it, it filled Bäni with anticipation as well. The soft cry of delight that Rusterholz uttered at the first bite was repeated six more times. Each ravioli was slightly different. Each filling was a new taste treat, and he couldn't name any of them. Nor did he try to solve the mystery. Thinking spoils pleasure, he liked to say. Everything in its own time.

"Delicatissimo," Bäni commended, as Maria took away the plates. She merely nodded expressionlessly. But she smiled when she saw her employer sitting there with his eyes closed, hands folded over his stomach, loudly smacking his lips.

"You have to show her," Rusterholz said after Maria had left the room. "She receives words stoically, like an artist accepting an award, flattered by the praise, yet doubting that he has been understood. You have to show your feelings, celebrate the meal. I happen to know that she often secretly observes me through the crack in the door, because she wants to experience how much I enjoy her creations. And if I smack my lips or clap my hands and break out in 'oohs' and 'ahs,' I sometimes hear her sobbing."

When Maria returned to place a new mystery before him, something the size of a fist, wrapped in grape leaves, Rusterholz rolled his eyes in expectation, like a child with a surprise package. With knife and fork he skillfully unveiled this next taste treat—he was certain that it would be one—and let out a little whistle of admiration on finding a quail wrapped in thin slices of bacon, as if he had discovered a enchanting girl veiled only in silk. And venturing on to the filling, which consisted of the bird's entrails, he again closed his eyes and waved his knife in the air like a baton, as if he wanted to put into music the harmony that his taste buds were experiencing.

Rusterholz stood beside his chair as Maria reappeared, and made a long, deep bow in her direction. She smiled again. He pushed another carafe toward Caesar; it was the third, and he poured himself a glass from the fourth. Then followed lamb and stuffed eggplant, and veal kidneys flambé with rice, and the fifth and sixth carafes were emptied.

"I enticed Maria away from Bacchus, and the old sot didn't even notice," Rusterholz said, raising his glass. "Long live Bacchus!"

"Long live all the gods, Wotan, Roman as well as Germanic," Bäni cried, slurring his words. "But down with all the heathen idols!"

Following a moment of ominous silence, Rusterholz burst out laughing, spraying the table with droplets that possessed all the excellent qualities of a Cabernet-Sauvignon. After he had wiped his nose and dried his eyes and halfway recovered from this act of God, Rusterholz brought his fist smashing down on the heavy wooden surface of the table like a thunderclap. "I told you not to say things like that when I'm drinking!"

Though readily ascribing the wordplay of his toast to his genius—"Götze" being the German word for "idol"—Bäni was nevertheless surprised at his pun and first looked as if he would pout, and then joined in Wotan's raucous laughter. "It's just that you drink so much I can never get a word in edgewise."

"So, to our godliness, Caesar, and to the Virgin

Maria, who is preparing our meal for us," Rusterholz roared, barely able to control himself now, and he emptied his almost full glass in one gulp. "Sometimes I actually ask myself whether or not she is a witch. You know, cooks are either saints or poisoners. It's true. I dreamed once that she was killing me. Not with poison—no, she was cooking course after course with ever-greater finesse, so that I would eat myself to death." And with great relish he tried to guess what Maria would serve next, what she had come up with to crown the evening. He loved to conclude a meal with something substantial, but delicate, of course, and he now considered what that might be. Nothing occurred to him. But at the moment Maria came through the door bearing a tray, he knew precisely that what he had wanted but could not name had arrived.

"Filetto di cinghiale al tartufo," Maria said, lifting the silver cover.

"Unbelievable," Rusterholz cried in delight, "she did it! Of all the thousands of dishes to choose from, this is the one I would have picked to finish with. Filet of wild boar with truffles. She knows me better than I know myself. What would my life be without you, Maria!"

Though Bäni demurred, saying it was impossible for him to take one bite more, Maria, at her master's orders, served him the wild boar, truffles, and plums.

"Think of the uniqueness of the creation, Caesar," Rusterholz said, attempting to sway his guest. "We are among the privileged, it is given to us and only us to know incomparable perfection. You cannot pass up this work of art, Caesar. You absolutely cannot."

"It's more like assassination by hydrochloric acid, like the Rubens painting in the Zurich Museum," Bäni said with a troubled smile.

"Now you've got it. But that's merely a fraction of the

whole truth, I fear. Listen, Caesar, even if this rare dish does eventually meet up with our gastric acids, the enzymes of pancreas and liver, and turn into shit, just think, it is our palates that the wild boar and black tubers enrich first. Only through our senses of smell and taste does it all become art. Do you understand?" And Rusterholz attacked the filet and truffles with knife and fork. "Eat, Caesar," he said between mouthfuls, "and become!"

"I can't, really. One bite, I'm afraid, and it would be the end." Bäni was pale under the white strands of hair that had fallen in his face.

"Well, then, I'll have to finish the masterpiece myself," Rusterholz said with an expression of both determination and self-contempt, as if it were sacrilege to leave even one bite. After a large gulp of wine and a big burp he pushed his plate to one side, pulled the platter over to him, and reached for the seventh and last carafe.

Bäni had to turn away. Even seeing Wotan eat, truffle sauce dripping from his mouth, was too much for him.

Rusterholz sat motionless behind the empty platter for a while, with only his digestive system making itself known from time to time, when he suddenly came to. "Now we shall canonize Maria once and for all," he announced, and filled his glass to the rim. Then he rose and began to sing in his powerful bass: "Sancta Maria, blessed among cooks!"

And Bäni, struggling to his feet, imitated in falsetto the response of thousands of believers on St. Peter's Square: "Ora pro nobis!"

Rusterholz continued, in the grand style that would have done a Russian Orthodox metropolitan proud: "Sancta Maria, sole provider of heavenly and hellish feasts," and "Sancta Maria, captivator of my soft and hard palate."

177

Bäni had to take a sharp breath to reach a falsetto for his "Ora pro nobis," for his swollen stomach was pressing hard on his diaphragm.

"Silenzio, voi bastardi intellettuali." Maria's low voice suddenly cut through the blasphemous devotional. Believing she had been summoned, she now stood in the doorway, trembling and crossing herself as if the devil himself were before her. Then she retreated, slamming the door hard behind her.

Rusterholz slapped his stomach and thighs, roaring with delight. His face turned dark red, almost the color of the Bordeaux, and Bäni whinnied along with him. The two raised their glasses once again. Rusterholz attempted a final toast, then drained his glass and threw it against the wall, where it shattered between two priceless Brupbacher engravings. Bäni felt obliged to follow suit, and his half-full glass fell just short of Wotan's pitch, hitting instead a rare hand-colored etching by Aschmann. He didn't even notice. The effort had knocked him back down onto his chair, which came very close to tipping over.

It had quieted down a bit—exhaustion seemed to be setting in—when Maria restored the mood. Bolting into the room with a silver tray in her hand, she threw it to the table with a crash, screaming, "Il mio ultimo pranzo per voi, divorate e andate all' inferno!" And in her dark vibrato her words sounded like a prophecy. She steamed off, resembling more an avenging angel than a saint, with Rusterholz applauding madly. On the tray lay the head of a rooster in its own blood, surrounded by a green circle of what appeared to be gallbladder.

"What did she say?" Bäni asked in shock.

"We should eat this and go to hell. She'll never cook

for us again." Rusterholz wiped the tears from his eyes. "She's a true daughter of Dante, is she not?"

"So she's quit," Bäni said worriedly, visibly affected by Maria's entrance.

"It happens occasionally. The last time was when I suggested we spawn a hermaphrodite together. A hermaphrodite that cooked for itself."

"Wotan, you're a pig," Bäni sputtered.

"That's right, and still she doesn't leave." Pulling himself up by the edge of the table, Rusterholz picked up the tray. "See, she is a witch. What did I tell you?" And he held out the tray to Bäni before he stumbled with it to the window and pitched it out into the darkness. Then he helped his friend to his feet and dragged him into the library, where he opened a bottle of Héritage Madame Ragnaud, a cognac whose grapes had ripened before his birth. Fumbling, he took two thick Davidoffs from his cigar case. "Helps the digestion, Caesar," he said, as he handed his friend the glass and a lit cigar.

22

When Manz called the clinic Thursday morning around ten, he was told that Professor Bäni had not yet arrived. Nor could he be reached at home, but his wife suggested he try calling Thalwil. Her husband had spent the previous evening with Rusterholz, where he usually slept over. No one answered at Rusterholz's, and at his department at the hospital they said he was not in, but was expected. They had not heard from him, however. At this, Manz decided to drive out to Thalwil to see for himself what he could find out about the two missing men.

A good fifteen minutes later Manz encountered Maria leaving the house with two suitcases and an overstuffed handbag. There was a malicious smile on her face as she confirmed that the professors were inside. She put down the cases and bag and willingly showed the policeman upstairs, first to the dining room, where the momentous mess of the spree of the night before was still evident. Manz inspected the bottles on the table with no little interest—they looked familiar, and he stepped closer to check the year. He was pleased by what he saw. The commissioner would not be able to dismiss this discovery, he told himself. The evidence against the gentlemen was slowly but surely growing more conclusive.

The impatience with which Maria indicated that he should follow her led to further surprises. Again he thought he saw her smile spitefully as she opened the door to the library. Manz drew back in horror. The sight of the two men lying on the floor between overturned chairs made him think for a moment that they were the victims of a violent crime, until it occurred to him what had happened. It could only have been the force of the Château Latour that had felled the two. Clearly there was no use asking questions, but Manz saw it as his duty at least to wake the men, to discover whether they were in need of medical assistance. Bäni, twisted into a strange position, wheezed loudly when Manz gave him a gentle nudge.

"Hey, you," came a croaking sound from behind Manz. He turned. Rusterholz, semiconscious, looked like a boxer trying unsuccessfully to get up after a heavy blow. His legs failed him. "Out!" Rusterholz bellowed. The swollen veins of his neck and temples, and his bushy eyebrows, drawn together over bloodshot eyes, made him look violent. "Get out of here!" He reached the chess table with effort and sat down, grabbing a few of the pieces and haphazardly throwing them in the direction of the intruder. "You've got no business here, you miserable shithead!"

Manz ducked as the next volley of chess pieces, aimed more carefully this time, flew by. He caught one reflexively—it was the black king—and stuck it in his pocket, more as a token than as evidence, and left the room as Rusterholz had advised.

Soon thereafter, Manz dropped Maria off at the Zurich train station with her bags. She told him she was leaving Rusterholz, for whom she had cooked for eight years now, as of that moment; she had never had a contract. But she didn't want to tell Manz the exact reason for her decision. He would have to be satisfied with what he had seen. He correctly surmised that this had not been the first such gluttonous spectacle. But the occasion for the drunkenness must have been a special one, he calculated. The wine, the year, attested to that.

Maria informed him that she would be at her sister's in Winterthur for a while; she was going to look for a new position from there. Would she go back to Italy? She had not decided yet. Only if she found a position where she had complete freedom. But that was unlikely in Italy. And she would no longer allow anyone to tell her what she was to cook.

23

After the car had disappeared around the corner, packed to the roof as it had been the Thursday before, Sonder went back into the house. The bare apartment, with only a few plain pieces of furniture left, should have made him sad, really, or at least reflective. But Sonder was content. He felt relief at each object he had given away, as if he were ridding himself of ballast. The missing curtains and lamp shades, and the dark squares on the wallpaper where pictures had hung, were visible signs to him that he was nearing his goal.

The only things he would have trouble parting with were still in the sitting room. There on the wall hung his weapons, untouched. Sonder had almost given in to the young couple's beseeching look at them. But despite their generous offer he could not bring himself to do so. He did not want these objects, which meant so much to him, to be put up for sale—the thought of people haggling over them depressed him. Robbed of their history, the bows and blowguns and spears would become nothing more than curiosities, decor for some modern apartment perhaps, in which the killing of animals would be discussed with a wrinkle of the nose by people who believed it was only the unscrupulous drives of human beings that kept animals from living together in peace. In the end he had allowed them to take the skulls of the chamois and bucks, which he long since had ceased to regard as trophies. He had presented them to the couple at no charge.

Just as Sonder was intending to take the weapons down from the wall and pack them in a crate, the doorbell rang. He opened the door, having no idea who would be visiting him at this hour, and was surprised to see Commissioner Häberli standing before him.

"Good evening, Herr Sonder, how are you?" Häberli said. "I was just in the neighborhood and thought I'd look in on you. I hope I'm not disturbing you."

"No, no, not at all," Sonder replied, relieved at the commissioner's friendly greeting. "Please, come in." And he led his visitor through the empty apartment out to the garden. He didn't miss Häberli's quick glance through the open doors of the sitting room.

"You'll be wondering what led me to come see you," the commissioner began, when they had taken a seat outside.

"Yes, of course."

"I'd like to have a little talk with you. I don't want it said later that I just let you . . . go away. . . . I almost said 'escape.' So that you understand me correctly," he quickly added at seeing the question on Sonder's face, "It has to do with my alibi this time, not yours."

Sonder didn't immediately understand what the commissioner was getting at, but was happy to see that his smile was friendly, and found it best simply to listen.

"I hear that tomorrow is your last day at work."

"Yes, that's true."

"And you're leaving soon on a trip?"

"On Sunday," Sonder said.

"It doesn't look as if you intend to return," Häberli ascertained, with a nod at the apartment.

"Yes, that's true."

"You can surely imagine what kind of speculation that will lead to if the press gets wind of it. I can imagine they might infer a connection between your departure and the death of Doctor Götze, assuming, of course, that the mystery is not solved beforehand. And I fear it won't come to that so quickly."

Sonder nodded. So that was it.

"You see," Häberli continued, "that is why I need an alibi confirming that I have dealt with you appropriately. They'll be after my head otherwise. And as I would like to keep our conversation as pleasant as possible, more private than professional, I came to see you out here this evening."

Sonder now understood what this was about, and saw no reason to doubt the commissioner's sincerity. "Would you like a beer? Please excuse me for not offering you one earlier."

"Gladly, if you're having one yourself."

When Sonder reached the kitchen it occurred to him that he no longer owned any glasses. But Häberli assured him that he didn't mind drinking from the bottle, he had always done so in the past. The two men clinked bottles with a smile—a casual observer might have thought that the two, who were roughly the same age, were school friends toasting old times.

Soon they were in animated conversation, telling each other about their lives. It turned out that they both came from rural areas, and they discussed what had brought each of them to Zurich. Häberli explained that he had become a policeman only because his elder brother had taken over their father's pig-fattening enterprise. And

Sonder talked about his butchcr shop, and the premature
deaths of his wife and child. He later brought up his
illness and operation, and mentioned the odds that the
doctors had given him. Of the two versions, he chose the
least optimistic, that of Götze, who had put it down in
black and white.

Häberli had held off with the question of what Sonder
planned to do next. A question that had already been
answered, in view of the empty apartment. He had assumed that Sonder would bring this up himself. But he
hadn't. Häberli's interest was not only of a personal nature. It was good for a commissioner to have information
on all the facts surrounding a murder case. When Sonder
now revealed his plans without beating around the bush,
Häberli was a little surprised. He hadn't reckoned on
this. Nor was it easy for him to understand that someone would wish to spend what time was left him in a
strange land. He himself usually went north for his vacation, and a journey down the Nile fifteen years before
had been the only trip he had taken outside of Europe.
But he was not one to discredit other people's ideas. And
he admitted to himself that if he weren't so afraid of
flying, he surely would have seen more of the world.
Looking at it more closely, he even admired Sonder. He
found that those people who put their ideas into action
made the most interesting contemporaries.

"And you plan to go hunting again in Africa?" Häberli asked, referring to the weapons he had seen on his
brief glance into the drawing room.

Sonder shook his head vehemently. He had been a
passionate hunter at one time, he explained. He had
hunted for sport, or better yet, as folklore; he had learned
it from his father and carried it on without thinking, as
a family tradition, so to speak. And for a long time there

had been no reason for him to question hunting, until a drastic event had forced him to view it from a different angle. But he was not opposed to hunting, Sonder continued, without mentioning the particular event; he simply felt different about it. As he saw it today, only those people who were particularly knowledgeable about nature and its interrelationships—which of necessity connoted a deep respect for every living thing—were entitled to kill. The instinct to kill demanded something additional of man, for man was capable of empathy. And empathy was the appropriate emotion, he found. It allowed man to compensate for the drive that nature had bequeathed him.

Häberli was silent, impressed by what Sonder had said. And when Sonder got up to go into the house, he followed him into the drawing room uninvited. Sonder removed each weapon from its wall mount, identified the country and place each had come from and what it had been used for, and often told a little story about it, after which he laid the weapon in the crate standing ready. He jumped from Asia to South America to Africa, and back to Asia. He ascended from the jungle to the highlands, and lost himself in the steppes only to find himself in another jungle again. He roved back and forth across countries and cultures, finding himself equally at home everywhere. He never became confused or had to correct himself. When he got to the projectile he had used as his quill, he remarked merely that he had found it in Africa and proceeded immediately to the blowpipe from the Amazon. He also mentioned Ricardo.

Häberli listened attentively, asking a question now and then, and this made Sonder happy, for the commissioner showed that he knew something about the topic —what a sloth looked like, for example.

187

When there was nothing left on the wall but nails, hooks, and wire, strange ciphers in the fading light of evening, Sonder turned to the three guns hanging on the adjacent wall. He took his father's hunting rifle down first, then his carbine, and leaned both against the crate without saying much about either. The precise movements with which Sonder took his own hunting rifle down last reminded Häberli of a ritual, and this impression was strengthened when Sonder carried the gun outside in both hands. There he sat down and laid the rifle across his lap.

"It was a long time ago, a very long time, that I last went hunting," he began, when Häberli had again sat down in his chair. "I was living in the Rhine Valley at the time. But I can remember that day as if it were yesterday. It was autumn, it was drizzling slightly, and I was alone, on my way to a forest clearing on the trail of a buck. I had spotted him there several times. But suddenly I saw a wild boar standing at the end of a hedge. It was an imposing animal, a powerful boar with great, dangerous tusks. It hadn't noticed me yet." Sonder's words were measured and his voice muffled, giving his listener the feeling that he wasn't being addressed directly, or perhaps exclusively. "And suddenly I felt a longing, a powerful longing I had never felt before. I wanted this animal. I felt somehow that it wouldn't be the same experience as shooting a buck or a chamois. He stood there, rooted to the ground, as I raised my weapon, majestic, if that can be said of a boar. And I believe he caught a whiff of me at the moment I pointed my gun at him. I shouldn't have fired, not then. I was probably overly anxious. I can't explain it otherwise. I was a good rifleman. It should have been a shot to the chest." Häberli saw how Sonder's right hand glided over the weapon, trembling lightly as if he were stroking it. "It didn't even bring him to his knees, though the blast swung him around. He stood facing me, looking at me with his tiny, hate-filled eyes. He snorted threateningly and then he attacked. I fired a second shot quickly; it hit him, but to no effect. Yes, I think I even saw the bullet bounce off his forehead. There then followed a terrible blow. I couldn't get out of the way fast enough. My knee was shattered, I couldn't get up, and my rifle lay on the ground out of my reach. But the boar, too, was lying on the ground, not thirty yards away. He was panting heavily and bits of red foam were flying through the air as he tossed his head from side to side." Sonder coughed. "I knew then that I had hit him in the lung. So it could only be a matter of time." Sonder coughed again, as if something were strangling him. "It must be terrible to suffocate. I wanted to set him free. But when I dragged myself over to my rifle and almost had my hands on it, I saw that the animal had gotten up. It was coming for my legs again with its last strength. It stood there swaying, wheezing loudly . . ." Sonder was overcome by a coughing fit. He put his hand to his chest, over his scar, and Häberli saw Sonder's ribcage rise and fall. But before he could reach over and help him—he wanted to thump him on the back—Sonder continued, gasping, his voice strained. "Wanted to reload. But couldn't. He attacked again. I pointed the gun at him. Ridiculous. But he didn't strike. He stumbled and lay near me, motionless." Sonder sank back into his chair, then grabbed his beer and took a long gulp that he held in his mouth for a while. "He fought with the last bit of air in his foaming lungs."

"And you never went hunting again?" Häberli asked, after a pause.

"No, not even after my leg got better. I found no

pleasure anymore in shooting rabbit or deer. The boar had not been afraid—he had defended himself."

"You should have gone after a boar again!"

Sonder smiled, shrugging his shoulders. "Perhaps." Suddenly he held out the weapon to the commissioner, indicating that he should take it. Häberli examined it as well as he could in the dim evening light. He wasn't sure what he was supposed to do with it. Embarrassed, he weighed it in his hands and sighted through the visor, aiming at a lit window. He knew a bit about weapons, but only what his work demanded.

"Please, take it," Sonder said. "Keep it."

Häberli was astonished at the offer. "I—yes, but why should it be me . . ."

"I'm asking you, please, take it. It would make me happy if you would take all of my weapons."

"But I don't understand. . . . Why me . . . ?"

"Because you now know that each one has a history. You're the only one besides me who knows these stories. And if you give a weapon away, then tell whoever it is that the thing has a history, that it's part of another story. I beg you, take the weapons. What am I to do with them otherwise?"

It was late when the two of them carried the crate out of the building, along with the rifles and the long blowgun, and put them in the commissioner's car. They could make room for the blowgun only by sticking part of it out the window.

24

Sonder set off for work that morning for the last time. For the last time he climbed the tree-shaded steps to the clinic, and as he looked out over the city he was conscious of the fact that he would be doing many things that day for the last time. He had thought about this day often in years past, but he had imagined it differently. He had no desire to go from office to office, from lab to lab, to be wished health and happiness. He was completely satisfied with the idea of the small farewell celebration to be held that afternoon.

Sonder went directly to the library. It was important to him to finish the task that Thalmann had suggested, rather than ordered him to do, though he had approached it without any great enthusiasm. He believed he could finish it that morning with a little effort. He refused to be interrupted as he recorded book titles and authors on index cards. Even Pat was able to get his attention for a few minutes only. By the time Sonder went to lunch all of the cards were filed alphabetically. He planned to return that afternoon to be sure the project was completed. Otherwise, there was nothing left for him to do. And he felt that even that job was unnecessary.

He arrived in the lunchroom early as usual, one of

the first, ate a bowl of soup alone, and then went out for a walk. It was what he always did, rain or shine.

On the way back to the library he suddenly felt an urge to stop by the autopsy room. He had avoided the place after his return from the sanatorium, since someone else had assumed his job. But now, only hours before his final departure, something prompted him to take one last look at his previous domain. Now, with his time running out, with his responsibilities receding from minute to minute, the danger of intruding on Zimmerli's space was also receding. But he would never be just another visitor there, no matter how little claim he had to it. Comparisons were inevitable; Sonder didn't question that.

It looked as it always had. He felt the sterility that emanated from the white-tiled room. He could smell it. Sonder was affected by the coolness, remembering how it had disturbed him on his first day there. The metal tables gleamed as always. His fingers trailed along the shelves, sought contact with table edges as he walked back and forth in the room. Had anyone asked what he was feeling, Sonder would not have been able to express it. He didn't know what it was that connected him to this space; perhaps it was merely the work he had performed here. He had never been particularly enthusiastic about it, could never be enthusiastic about working on corpses. But he had honestly tried to perform his duties well, and had been appreciated, at least until Götze appeared. Götze never refrained from raising his voice, not even in the presence of the dead. Sonder enjoyed the peaceful quiet that ruled here once again.

"I'm glad you've come!" Zimmerli rushed toward Sonder and shook his hand. "How many years was it?"

"Thirty-two."

"A long time," Zimmerli said, and nodded appreciatively. "I imagine it will be the same with me."

They talked for a while. Zimmerli answered Sonder's question whether he had a lot of work at the moment in the negative. The weather was too nice to die in, he said. Sonder agreed, smiling. But he did have one more patient, Zimmerli said. He asked Sonder to stay, asked him, as he wheeled the body into the room, if he would like to perform one last autopsy. Sonder refused, thanking him, but said he would like to sit in the corner and watch from a distance. Sonder was pleased by the quiet way Zimmerli went about his work, cutting open the body without inappropriate comment. Most people were unable to leave it at that, doctors included. Sonder had never understood it. He would not make comments even when gutting an animal.

At three o'clock they all met in the cafeteria. Everyone from the department was there, with the exception of Professor Bäni, who had not appeared at work the day before either. The rumor was that he was suffering from indigestion, probably a stomach virus. It was a nice party, though not totally diverting, which had less to do with the tragic circumstances than with the fact that for many of them, Sonder was marked by death. Despite his apparent good health.

As they were having coffee and cake, Director Arpagaus addressed a few words of thanks to Sonder. He was a loyal, responsible colleague, he said, and praised the courage with which he had withstood his recent test, and in the name of the entire clinic staff wished him much happiness in his well-deserved retirement. With this Arpagaus presented Sonder with a gold watch, a symbol—as he put it—of a long and happy time to come.

Doctor Thalmann, in the name of Professor Bäni and the department, thanked Sonder for the expert and excellent work he had performed, for his dependability, and, above all, for his collegiality. He had assisted many young pathologists in his always accommodating manner, Thalmann said, offering them valuable advice, as Professor Bäni would have it. He closed by saying that it had not been easy to decide what to give a man who loved to travel and who was not the least interested in retiring, and then bestowed on him a pocketknife and a flask that, at Pat's suggestion, had been filled with kirsch. "May this, dear Herr Sonder, be a happy reminder of your homeland and also of those of us in the department. I assure you that we will be thinking of you often."

Director Arpagaus, baffled, looked first at Thalmann, then at Sonder. But before he could ask for an explanation he was called to the phone. It was urgent. He quickly took his leave of Sonder and hurried to his office, only to find out that Professor Bäni had been taken to the hospital an hour earlier.

25

If Commissioner Häberli changed the hour of his usual Sunday morning reflection to the evening before, it was for good reason. He intended to go to the airport on Sunday to say good-bye to Gottfried Sonder. He felt he owed him that. It had been two weeks since he had met Sonder, but it was as if he had known the man for years. He wasn't sure why this was so, but he had been trying to decide why since his recent visit. It occurred to him that it wasn't Sonder's travel stories that had impressed him so, but rather the way in which he described his experiences. Sonder himself was never the center of them, as was usually the case with travel stories. No, it was the foreign hunter whose courage and skill Sonder talked about, or the animal being hunted. He himself was always only the quiet observer, thinking his thoughts. And what strange thoughts they were—few people would ascribe them to such a modest man. Even in his description of his own battle with the wild boar, it obviously was more important to him to create respect for the animal than to emphasize his own courage. Häberli valued Sonder's openness toward him as a sign of great personal trust—and then there were the weapons as well, which Sonder had given him and which, after all that he knew about the man, he did not view as a gift. They represented a kind of legacy that he was to hold in trust. Apparently he enjoyed Sonder's confidence. He wanted to return the compliment by seeing him off.

That Saturday evening Häberli sought out the cabin in the woods where the departmental party had taken place. He wanted to order his thoughts there, open himself to his creative impulses. At any rate, there was a connection between this place and Götze's case. Götze had been expected here—by Professor Bäni, among others, whose role in this whole affair he wished, or had, to consider today. There was reason to, today especially; the possibility of solving Götze's case by conventional means had worsened drastically with one blow, and Häberli was irritated. He had deliberately spared Bäni, had not let him know that he suspected him of involvement. The professor was to believe himself safe, for there was no way to shake his alibi without a mistake on his part. But now, after the orgiastic feast at Rusterholz's—Manz had told him about it—now, when he thought he had the professors where he wanted them, Bäni was out of the game and Rusterholz had disappeared. Thalmann had informed him that day that Bäni was in intensive care, unconscious, probably as the result of a cerebral hemorrhage. It didn't look good. This wasn't surprising, Thalmann said, as the professor's mental competence had diminished considerably of late. And Professor Rusterholz, in whose interrogation he had set great hope, had disappeared following his bizarre encounter with Manz. No one answered at his house, and he had not shown his face at the office since Wednesday. Both his cars were in the garage; they could be seen through the tiny window, Manz had reported. Manz had called all the airlines

for any information on a passenger by the name of Rusterholz. Without success.

Häberli didn't know why he was thinking of the wild
boar as he took the narrow path to the edge of the forest,
but he couldn't get Sonder's vivid description of it out of
his mind. He hadn't known until then that there were
wild boars in those woods, animals that under certain
circumstances could be dangerous. Häberli parked his
car by the woodpile, exactly where Bäni and Götze had
parked their cars only days before.

On his way to the cabin Häberli tried to picture Götze,
using what he had heard about him to envision him in
Bäni's company, to bring the two of them together in his
mind. As hopeless as things were—where was he to find
an answer to his questions?—he was forced to turn once
again to his tried and true method. He hoped to stumble
on some possible argument that might have taken place
between the two—on a motive, that was to say. But try
as he might, Häberli couldn't manage to bring the two
of them together. The defenseless body in the river refused to turn into the aggressive man Götze had been
described as being, and Bäni kept sliding into a
lethargic—not to say comatose—state. The real reason
for this failure was that the wild boar kept crashing into
the picture, preventing Bäni and Götze from coming to
life.

Häberli sat down on a bench somewhat off the path
close to the cabin to try a different approach. It wasn't
like him to give up so easily. He had to admit, though,
that this was neither the time nor the place to expend
further energy. But why, he asked himself, had his proven
method failed him today? Did the answer lie in himself?
And then, as he stepped back to include himself in the

analysis of this failure, he began to get angry. The point of the exercise had always been to gather inspiration from his surroundings. To force his ideas, no matter how crazy they seemed. And what had he accomplished thus far? He had insisted on suppressing the wild boar, continually pushing its way into the picture. He had been trying the whole time to avoid precisely what he was essentially striving for.

Scarcely had Häberli completed this thought than the boar once again forced his way into the foreground. The boar . . . followed by Sonder. Why not, Häberli thought. They stood facing each other, the hunter and the hunted, assailant and victim. Just as Sonder had related it. But to his great astonishment the figures wouldn't stay in their places, they began to overlap each other. Nor was Sonder as he would have been then, Häberli ascertained; he wasn't the young man with the crushed knee, no, he was the Sonder of today. They must have something in common, Sonder and the wild boar. Of course! They had both been wounded in the lung. But was that enough to call up such a strong image? Häberli doubted it. He decided to concentrate again on the hunter's encounter with the boar, in the dramatic way Sonder had described it. His powers of observation stood him in good stead now, and his memory had not diminished in the least. Yes, Häberli thought to himself, if anything, his senses had sharpened with age. Today, without effort, he could take in and retain even those things that were inessential.

At the moment that Sonder had mentioned the wounded and panting animal he had suffered a heavy coughing spell. And it now occurred to Häberli that Sonder had grabbed his chest, not his knee, when mentioning his own wound. That could mean that Sonder had taken the animal's role in the telling—he must have felt at one with the animal. Understandable, looked at from today. Both had injured lungs. But there was something else! When the boar hit the ground, hadn't Sonder believed that it was over? But the boar had attacked again. And Sonder, the Sonder of today, hadn't he said that for him it could only be a question of time? The medical report! Had Sonder too . . . ?

Häberli got a jolt that propelled his portly figure off the bench. He began hurrying along the path he had just taken, as if he were being chased. Actually, he was fleeing from a thought that had begun to crystallize, fearing it would grow and expand to become a dangerous image. He hurried anxiously past the hikers coming toward him, noticing them as little as he noticed the heat or the fact that he should be taking it easy, because of his heart. A feeling of dizziness brought him back to his senses. He walked slower now, his shirt sticking to his skin.

Suddenly he again felt irritated, less by his absurd notion than by the vehemence with which he fought it off, though he knew he couldn't get rid of it, that this germ of a thought would not be suppressed. Once he had thought it, it was thought! And even if the idea that Sonder was directly involved in the physician's death seemed more a product of his ineffectuality in solving Götze's case, he couldn't rid himself of it. It was, moreover, an idea that had to be pursued, thought out to the end— sooner or later, it demanded this of him.

It wasn't that it was difficult for Häberli to consider Sonder, upright citizen that he was, a suspect in his investigation. That belonged to his profession. No, he was shocked to feel that he might betray the trust that Sonder had placed in him should he pursue the thought that this man could be a murderer. Nor did it help to ask himself whether Sonder—were he guilty of, or involved in, the

199

crime—would have told him everything he did in so friendly a fashion. The commissioner would then have become his enemy, his hunter. But he was somewhat consoled by the thought. His body relaxed. He stopped, wiped the sweat from his face, looked around him and up at the thin treetops. He placated himself with the thought that Sonder would surely forgive this hint of suspicion; Sonder would surely understand that a good criminologist could not allow himself to separate private thoughts from professional.

The further Häberli distanced himself from that first sudden notion that fueled his terrible suspicion, the more certain he became that the case he was in the process of building lacked any foundation. He must have invented the whole thing, he told himself. Götze's case had him fumbling in the dark, and his imagination had run wild. There could be no other explanation, he would not allow it. If he continued with this line of thinking because he had to follow it to its logical end, his own feelings to the contrary, then he would only embarrass himself in the end. The way Sonder had told the tale expressed only a deep respect for the animal he had done battle with. There was nothing more to it.

Having arrived at the edge of the forest, Häberli sought out a quiet spot behind the pile of wood there and sat down on a tree stump. Despite a slight headache, which he blamed on the enormous mental and physical strain he was under, he caught his breath and again tackled the unavoidable. And scarcely had he closed his eyes and given his thought free rein when the same strong image again appeared, having lost none of its power despite his attempt to dismiss it. As he went over the hunting story once more, his previous suspicions were intensified, particularly by the fact that the two figures not only overlapped in the final, confused stage of the struggle, but turned into one another, merged. Sonder himself took on something of a hunted animal. Häberli again felt himself resist pursuing this line of thought. He was on the verge of giving the whole thing up and using his headache, which was growing ever stronger, to block any further projection of the image when something totally unexpected happened. What he had attempted an hour before—namely, to picture Götze—now occurred of its own accord. Sly and obnoxious, as the man had been described to him by different people, Götze suddenly stood in front of the wounded animal—now a mythical half-man, half-beast. And the creature seemed prepared to attack. Or was it more a defensive stance, in response to Götze's aggressive posture?

The commissioner was filled with a mixture of fascination and horror. He could not remember an image of such clarity ever appearing to him before. His doubts of the moment before faded. He could no longer dismiss what he had pictured as simply a crazy notion, not without deceiving himself. He had to give credence, after all, to the gift that had led to his numerous successes. If he now assumed that it was Sonder who had killed Götze, it was more than a mental game—even if there was not one single shred of evidence against Sonder, and his hypothesis rested alone on images wrested from his subconscious.

Sonder's alibi had holes in it, they knew that already. On top of which, Häberli now reflected, Sonder could have known that Götze would arrive at the party late. But that would mean that the murder had been committed here, here where he, Häberli, was now sitting. The slight chill that now came over him was not from the thought that a man had been killed here—Häberli was inured to that. No, he had been struck by the thought that on his arrival here, it was at precisely this spot that he had remembered the wild boar, and it was here, at the possible scene of the crime, that his clearest image now had appeared to him.

All that remained was the question of the murder weapon. The way Götze had died still remained unexplained, and after all the time that had elapsed, it was unlikely that they would ever find out. But if an answer were to be found, Häberli thought, the key—assuming there was some truth to his mental images—logically must lie in Sonder's tale. All the clues up to that point had derived from it. Sonder himself had furnished them, whether out of exaggerated naiveté or boundless trust. Häberli scarcely dared hope for Sonder's innocence now.

Once again he grappled with the story, this time at the decisive point of the boar's final attack. It occurred to Häberli now how often Sonder had mentioned the boar's lung, its foaming, blood-tinged breath. The animal had fought with its last bit of air. That's how Sonder had put it. It was possible that this description derived solely from a compassionate man's great sense of empathy. But Häberli did not discount a deeper significance, which he searched for, but could not find.

Häberli knew that he would fight the impulse to include in his calculations the collection of weapons that had been lying in his basement since Thursday evening. Weren't these weapons the strongest evidence of Sonder's trust in him? Weren't they a sure sign of Sonder's innocence? Häberli was disturbed by this. He began to ask himself whether he really needed to torture himself with it—hadn't he already done his duty? And he realized that any further meditation on his part would bring depressing results. The fact that it didn't take much to convince himself to deal with the issue of the weapons, to betray Sonder's trust, was a reflection of just how much a prisoner he was of his own mental processes.

In his mind he saw the rifles, the spears, the bows, the crossbows, the blowguns, the . . . blow! Lungs! Pipe! The metal pipe in Götze's car! The projectile! A pinprick, nothing more! His head spun with images, with objects. Metal pipes and projectiles circled one another, threatened to connect, connected. Häberli felt dizzy, the blood hammered mercilessly in his head, making the pain almost unbearable, carrying it on to his heart, his lungs, everywhere.

Häberli staggered to his car, sat down on the passenger seat, and leaned back in exhaustion. The last light of the sun, weak now, almost mild, fell through the open door onto his face. Slowly the pain subsided. Häberli felt drained and puffy and tired, as after a long, hot bath. His eyes closed; he felt the sun going down. The projectile lay in his basement, the pipe was at the office. And he knew that what he felt was anything but triumph. He drove home slowly.

The shrill ringing of the telephone startled him out of a troubled sleep. It was dark. He was lying on his bed, still fully clothed. Manz apologized for disturbing him at such a late hour; he was calling with the latest news. Professor Rusterholz had been found, he said, in his wine cellar, lying beneath an overturned rack. He must have gone on a rampage. It seemed that he had smashed hundreds of bottles against the wall before the accident happened. Häberli was no longer listening as Manz described how blood had mixed with the wine on the floor, and didn't laugh when Manz said that, in addition to a body drowned in water, they had a body drowned in wine in the basement. Häberli's thoughts were elsewhere. He was preoccupied with the consequences of Rusterholz's death.

What did Manz make of the fact, Häberli wondered after he had hung up, that he had not reacted at all to the news? At the same time he questioned whether he hadn't made a mistake in letting Manz know that Sonder was leaving the next day. It might have been all right had he not asked Manz to accompany him to the airport. No, he hadn't asked, it had been more an order. "Don't you have time . . . ?" That could prove a fatal mistake. If only Manz hadn't called! Häberli sank down onto the bed with a loud sigh. What if Manz made a move to keep Sonder from leaving, held him for questioning? In his present condition it could mean Sonder's collapse—guilty or not. And wasn't that like passing sentence on Sonder, something he would have to take responsibility for? He might be making a mistake that could never again be rectified. Sonder a murderer? No, he wasn't a murderer. Murderers were different! But how to stop what he himself had set in motion? He had put Manz on the trail. And thus had taken the decision out of his own hands. On a case like this!

26

S onder didn't need to look back to know that the eyes
of the few people in the tram followed him as he
got out. The large backpack he was carrying was reason
enough to stare at an old and limping man, with amusement at first, then with a shake of the head when they
noticed that he was heading for the bridge where the
tram would have taken him anyway, in the direction of
Bellevue. But Sonder had never been particularly concerned with the pitying smiles of the smug citizenry, and
on this Sunday he even enjoyed them. He stood at the
rail in the middle of the bridge and looked out over the
lake. The view was a familiar one. He often had gotten
off at Bürkli Square to walk over the bridge and stand
precisely at this point to look at the view. The city was
barely visible from here. It was easy to imagine it away.
He had stood here in sunlight and in snowfall, in fog and
drizzle, in the dawn of a fall morning and during the
föhn season, when the mountains beyond the deep blue
lake became crystal clear and looked like a huge backdrop. And today it seemed to Sonder that everything was
a backdrop. The mountains looked as unreal as the
houses had on Bahnhofstrasse. Yes, it was as if everything, everything he knew, everything he had experi-

enced, here and in those mountains, was losing its reality.

From Bellevue he took the tram along the Limmat Quay to the train station. The images flew by as in a film, the Limmat with its bridges, the tower of Saint Peter's, the guildhalls, the empty space left behind by the meat market, and the cranes as well, there were so many of them. So this is it, Sonder thought, standing straddle-legged at the station as he swung the pack onto his back. This was his farewell to the city that had provided him with work for many years, and asylum as well, though not much more. The train would take him to Kloten, to the airport, and from there he would fly to Africa. And as he thought about it he felt Africa begin to lose much of its dreamlike quality and slowly become reality.

Bruno Thalmann didn't notice Pat until she was standing right in front of him. "Caesar is dead," he said in a muted voice. "His wife called me."

Pat thought that Bruno looked even paler than usual, even more fragile. Like a violinist, she thought. "Everything is moving so quickly all of a sudden."

"Yes," Thalmann said softly. They stood there for a while without moving, stunned, out of place in the ebullient chaos of the airport.

"Come on, let's go see Göpf Sonder." Pat took Thalmann's arm. "For him, life will go on."

"What do you think, should we tell him?" Thalmann asked as they took the escalator up.

"No, let's leave it. Unless he asks about Caesar."

Thalmann nodded silently.

"Do you think I'll have problems with my dissertation now?" Pat asked later, on their way to the departure terminal.

"No, I'm sure you won't."

They had arranged to meet Sonder in the cockpit, a bar in the upper part of the terminal. "He's here already," Pat called as they came to the stairs, and she hurried them up nimbly. Thalmann remained at a distance behind.

Manz stood not far from the spot where Pat Wyss had met Bruno Thalmann, reading an article on the international fencing tournament in Milan. He occasionally lowered the newspaper to keep an eye out for the commissioner—surprised, for it was unusual for Häberli to be late. He was impatient as well, for he had another piece of startling news. As the minutes passed, Manz asked himself if there had been a misunderstanding, if Häberli perhaps was waiting for him somewhere else with the same impatience. He was just folding up the paper with the intention of looking for the commissioner when he spotted him in the midst of a group of Japanese tourists on the escalator. Häberli apologized. He blamed his delay on the miserable night he had had, a night spent more on his balcony than in his bed. Manz waved it off. Häberli didn't need to say anything. He was tired, that was easy to see. But he also seemed strangely restless. He headed immediately for the departure terminal.

"I called Maria today and told her that Rusterholz is dead," Manz said bluntly.

"And?"

"At first she seemed truly moved, and blamed herself. She shouldn't have left him, she said, then it wouldn't have happened. But then she began to criticize him. She said it was his own fault that it had come to this. But she didn't want to talk about that Wednesday evening at first.

Only when I told her about Bäni did she start talking. And what she had to say is revealing."

"I'm listening," Häberli said, as Manz paused.

"That Wednesday, Bäni apparently arrived at Rusterholz's quite late, and unexpected. His clothing was wet and muddy, she said. That night she, together with Rusterholz, cleaned his suit and the car. It was completely covered in mud as well. So his alibi was contrived. They made it up. And everything points to the fact that Bäni was on the Sihl that evening. Otherwise they wouldn't have needed to cook up this scheme." Manz looked at the commissioner expectantly.

"So, so," was all Häberli had to say. He had stopped at the big board to look for the flight to Dar-es-Salaam. When he couldn't find it he left Manz—who had expected somewhat more than a "so, so"—standing there and went to the information desk. There he found out that it was a charter flight that would be departing from Terminal A.

"We'll probably be drinking a champagne toast today," Häberli said, as they continued on their way.

"What? You mean the case is solved?" Manz looked at his boss in disbelief.

"Perhaps not, but probably closed."

"I'm not quite following you." Manz didn't understand how Maria's statement, which had really added nothing new, but rather had solidified a long-held suspicion, could suddenly bring Häberli to such a conclusion. In going over the various scenarios of this murder, how often had he included Bäni in them, had particularly stressed his involvement? Häberli must know more than he was saying if he was now deciding to close the case. He could scarcely be content with the facts with which he—Manz—was familiar. "But Bäni and Rusterholz aren't enough. There had to have been at least one other person involved."

"That's possible." Häberli's consensus seemed indifferent. He was occupied elsewhere, looking around in all directions.

"Sonder," Manz suddenly murmured. That's why we're here! "Sonder?" he repeated now in an inquisitive undertone. It was suddenly clear to Manz why he had been asked along this morning. He should have known. Häberli didn't do anything without good reason. Sonder! So it was he and the professors. He himself had suspected this, and had let Häberli know it. But Häberli had been against the idea. Why the switch now? "So you believe he's the man we're after!"

Pat suppressed a cry when she saw the two policemen. She involuntarily reached for Sonder, her fingers clawed his arm. Sonder was startled when he looked at her, and his eyes followed hers down to the terminal. Pat couldn't understand the smile that crossed his face. She couldn't understand how he could sit there quietly and surrender his fate to these bloodhounds. Her head raced with ideas of how she might put the police off the trail, how she might enable Sonder to get through passport control without being detained. She was fiercely determined to do everything she could to secure his departure; she even thought of throwing herself dramatically down the stairs to draw everyone's attention to her. Sonder shook his head almost imperceptibly, as if he had read her thoughts. Only then did Pat let go of his arm.

"Things will happen as they must," Sonder said softly.

Her adamant "no" caused Thalmann to look up in

surprise. He seemed to have noticed nothing of what was
going on around him. Nor could he have imagined any
greater danger to this retiree than his flight from medical
care. "No," Pat repeated, more quietly this time, but still
vehement. But when Sonder waved to the commissioner,
who was still looking around, she began to doubt her
suspicions. She asked herself if her observations had been
mistaken. But why else would the police be here? It was
obvious. They were looking for him! And Häberli now
had discovered Sonder and was waving back.

Pat closely watched the two policemen down in the
terminal. She would have given anything to have been
able to hear what they were saying. Adrian seemed engrossed, almost indignant, while the commissioner appeared rather helpless, making gestures that appeared
almost appeasing—at least that was how she interpreted
their behavior. And when the two men finally came up
the steps, Pat found herself holding her breath.

Bruno Thalmann, who viewed the presence of the
police as coincidental, was the first to rise when Häberli
and Manz approached the table, and he moved his chair
over closer to Sonder's before the commissioner even
asked if they could sit down.

"But of course!" Sonder said this so naturally that
Pat involuntarily looked first at Häberli and then at
Manz. "You see," her eyes seemed to say, "Göpf Sonder
isn't afraid of you." She moved somewhat closer to Son-
der herself, so that she was seated between him and
Häberli, across from Manz.

"Your big day," the commissioner said to Sonder with
a smile.

"Yes, you could say that."

"Travel fever?"

"Less so than usual."

THE WILD BOAR

The desultory conversation between Häberli and Sonder didn't conceal the tense mood at the table. With the exception of Thalmann they all knew how critical the next half hour would be, they all felt how serious the consequences. Not only for Sonder. Even an onlooker could have recognized that something important was going on here, judging from how those at the table were watching each other, how they were avoiding each other's eyes while at the same time aping innocence or ignorance. An elegantly dressed man, gray at the temples, who was sitting at the table behind Manz, picked up the tension, at least. For some time now he scarcely had been able to take his eyes off Pat. He had followed the changes in her expression and would have put money on the likelihood that her eyes, which at first expressed pleasure, then anger and fear, would soon have tears flowing from them, for whatever reason.

What did Pat know? Manz asked himself over and over. He no longer doubted that she was trying to protect Sonder. She was certainly not making Manz's task any easier. He wanted to act without bias, as far as that was still possible. His feelings for Pat should not enter into it. Otherwise he had failed, most of all himself. It would mean that he was capable of being blackmailed. And Pat was giving him no choice in the matter. Her behavior, if it didn't prove Sonder's guilt, was certainly making it probable. What was left but for him to question Sonder? At the risk, of course, of making a fool of himself. Sonder had the advantage, naturally. Time was on his side. Manz's questions would have to be sharp if they were to bring results. But it would be catastrophic to detain Sonder now as a suspect, to keep him from his journey without being able to prove anything later. As Häberli had just explained to him, it could have unpleasant repercussions, for Sonder primarily, but for himself as well. Manz was not only thinking of his career. On the other hand, he wouldn't be totally satisfied if he succeeded in proving Sonder's guilt either. It wouldn't have been he who had collared Sonder—it was Häberli who had put Manz on the trail. And Häberli was leaving it to him to decide what to do. He wouldn't fault him, no matter what, Häberli had told him. And the way he was chatting with Sonder now, he appeared genuinely not to want to influence events one way or the other. But why had Häberli asked him to come with him? To take care of the unpleasant part? Or was it, in the end, a kind of test?

"Are you here in a professional capacity?" Thalmann asked, having scarcely participated in the conversation up to that point.

"Yes," Manz answered. And Thalmann was surprised at how quiet it suddenly became at the table. Pat's eyes flashed disdainfully.

Everyone looked at Manz. "How is Professor Bäni?" he asked.

The question was unexpected. By everyone. "He died last night," Pat answered quickly, and was immediately angry at herself that she hadn't let Bruno Thalmann be the one to respond.

"Rusterholz is dead as well," Manz said. "He was a friend of Professor Bäni's, wasn't he?"

"But surely there's no connection," Thalmann interjected worriedly.

"According to Rusterholz's statement, Professor Bäni spent the entire evening following the departmental party with him. We found out today that this isn't true. He arrived only very late that evening. Totally covered in mud. It was the evening on which we assume Doctor Götze was taken to the Sihl."

"What is that supposed to mean?" Thalmann looked from Manz to Häberli in astonishment. The commissioner remained silent.

"There is much that is still left unexplained," Manz answered. "There must be someone who could tell us something about it. We're looking for him."

Pat shuddered. Her hope that the topic of Bäni and Rusterholz would divert the conversation was crushed. Manz was simply preparing the final blow. Now danger was imminent. "Bruno Thalmann and I have come here to say good-bye to Göpf Sonder." The adamant tone in her voice, and her jutting chin turned Pat's statement into a reproach. "We don't have much time left." Her hand sought something to hold on to, sought the strong hand of Sonder under the table—unnoticed, she thought. But for some time now no movement at the table had gone unobserved. "We can discuss everything else later."

"Yes, that's true," Thalmann agreed, visibly irritated that he had asked the police what they were doing there. And Manz thought he saw Häberli nod in agreement. He had to assume that Pat was not going to let go, that she would leave with Sonder if he persisted. What could he do, hold him without a warrant? When his eyes met Pat's, he believed that he saw for one brief moment an imploring expression in them, more a plea than a threat. And then she turned quickly to Sonder again. And Sonder? He seemed unaffected by what was going on around him, seemed calm, radiating the dignity of the great fir tree. Was it Häberli's behavior, Sonder's calm, Pat's determined resistance, or all these things together? Manz didn't know what was robbing him of the strength to do what he believed had to be done.

When Sonder got up, saying it was time for him to leave, Manz stood up as well. More quickly than the others. And as he took the hand that Sonder extended to him with disarming naturalness, he was incapable of saying anything intelligent. A murmur, a handshake, nothing more. He stood there helplessly looking at Häberli in expectation. But the commissioner didn't seem to notice—no, he even clapped the man on the shoulder as if he were expressing admiration. Next came Thalmann, shaking his head slightly as he wished Sonder well. It had the effect of a gentle scolding. Pat, however, had walked around the table, where she waited for Sonder. She put her arm through his and accompanied him down the stairs.

Four pairs of eyes followed the strange pair, including those of the man at the next table, who believed he had lost his imaginary bet, though he continued to follow the scene with interest.

"Göpf, you can't imagine how afraid I was." Pat whispered though they were out of earshot.

"Yes, yes, I know. I could only be as calm as I was because of you."

Pat didn't understand. But understanding was unimportant to her at the moment. Göpf Sonder had made it, he was free. That was all that counted now. "Will you write to me?"

"Yes, if you wish."

At the passport counter Pat put her arms around the old man. "Göpf . . ."

"Thank you for everything," Sonder said. "I'll never forget how you fought for me." He extricated himself from her embrace when he felt the tears on her cheeks and hurried to the exit, searching awkwardly for his passport and boarding card.

To Manz, who had watched the scene, it was as if

Sonder were fleeing something. Only now, for the first time. And Pat too was disappearing from view, hurrying away without even turning back to look at Sonder again. Manz glanced at the commissioner questioningly. What else could we have done? Häberli's expression seemed to say.

Fifteen minutes went by before Pat reappeared. She cheerfully greeted the stranger, who smiled at her benevolently on the stairs.

"Perhaps this is not the time for a little celebration," Häberli said, as Pat walked up to the table. "But I'd like to invite everyone to a glass of champagne."

Thalmann wasn't so disposed. "I'm not in the mood," he said, "and I have to go, anyway." He stood up to leave as Pat was sitting down again.

"Clouds are gathering, it looks like a storm," Pat said, after a moment's silence.

"High time," Häberli responded.

"It hasn't rained since the night Götze was dumped in the Sihl." Manz had to admit that his statement was a banal one, considering everything that had happened since, the deaths of the professors and Sonder's departure.

When the waiter brought the champagne they all clinked glasses, smiling, but silent. They were thinking of Sonder, each of them, and each knew that the other two were as well. But no one proposed a toast. No one was prepared to risk taking on the ballast they had just cast off. Pat's smile was enchanting, Manz found, as it had been before all of this had started. He was still rattled, he was still struggling with his feelings, but he already knew that he would see Pat again, and not only at the health club. The hint of a twinkle in her eyes told him

this. And Häberli? He had decided to retrieve the projectile from its crate in the basement that very day, and
destroy it. He wanted to avoid the temptation of testing
it in the metal pipe. The memory of Sonder would enable
him to endure this mystery, he thought.